FOREST
WOLF

FOREST WOLF

Bernadette Cornette

[Le loup des stups, translated from French by Pacita Consuelo L Maaliw]

FOREST WOLF

Copyright © 2015 by Editions Dedicaces LLC

All rights reserved. No part of this book may be used or
reproduced in any form
whatsoever without written permission except in the
case of brief quotations
embodied in critical articles or reviews.

Published by:
    Editions Dedicaces LLC
    12759 NE Whitaker Way, Suite D833
    Portland, Oregon, 97230
    www.dedicaces.us

Library of Congress Cataloging-in-Publication Data
    Cornette, Bernadette.
    Forest Wolf / by Bernadette Cornette.
    p. cm.
    ISBN-13: 978-1-77076-512-2 (alk. paper)
    ISBN-10: 1-77076-512-3 (alk. paper)

Contents

PREFACE

Of course, whodunits, everyone has read them, and the genre's success was far from dying out. However, it does not mean in any way that its inspiration cannot be reinvented; and that was what was being done by Bernadette Cornette in *Forest Wolf*.

The first point of originality in this whodunit, one that captures the eye, was that it does not look like a whodunit, but a simple slice-of-life novel. However, the atmosphere was very present, captivating, mysterious, and stubbornly calls for a rediscovery to be followed until the end. As for the protagonists, and of course for that of the main character, they are not just front-liners; neither are they officers, detectives, nor journalists. They have no trace of being your typical investigators. They are simply just like the ordinary everyday people we see in the streets, sometimes quite literally so, as the main character was a homeless person. That said, they are just nameless faces, humans bearing the characteristics of the species, nothing more.

It's no small feat, of course, to successfully captivate the reader by just using situations and characters with such ordinary features. The ability to mingle the ordinary with the exciting was not a skill easily within reach of every writer. However, the whole package, as with the style and the elements of intrigue, run to this level of excellence.

With characters that ride the merry-go-round of a Cornelian drama and a Racinian tragedy – somewhat jolted by uncontrollable events, or voluntarily plunging into a tragedy, we can certainly look forward to a moving and passionate story.

I will thus say no more, so as to leave the readers the pleasure of discovering a whodunit very much unlike the others.

Thierry ROLLET
Literary agent

CHAPTER I

He was for sale in the workforce market. In the selection process, he was evaluated, registered among those above fifty-five years old, and he was sent aside among the waiting list of recyclable materials. He ended up with a taker: he was to be a caretaker.

He had an appointment with a Bérengère Salvignol, sole proprietor of building number 9, Rue du Vau-L'Eau. The pedantic woman laid on the saccharine as she laid out his work for him. 'I expect you to have absolute availability for my tenants. That was included in our contract as custodian.' she concluded. She avoided using 'caretaker' – a bad word. It was just as if a sweeper became a surface technician, or the postman as an agent. She annoyed him. 'And just how do you call stuffed turkey in your language to the prejudiced?' was what he wanted to ask her. He would just lose his job even before he started. Besides, this Bérengère looked like one of those who would file a complaint for aggravated misogyny. He just wanted her to leave already. The more she talked, the more she fretted, the less he listened as he was just nauseous from her perfume. The smell was so musky, that he could swear that he saw a skunk in heat going around the room. It had nothing to do with the squashed ramalama. 'I think I've covered everything. Voilà, voilààà!' she chimed, finally. No, he had no questions. Yes, he will call if there were any problems. Goodbye.

Now that she has left the office – his office – he can finally claim the space, and air it out.

Street-side: a rectangular room a dozen square meters big, furnished with a brownish velvet couch, a coffee table made out of natural pine, and a closet with overlapping sliding doors. The kitchenette carried the essentials: tiles, fridge, water heater, sink, a small table, and two folding chairs. In the alcove covered by a mustard yellow satin curtain was a bed for two and rattan nightstand.

Courtyard-side: bathroom with toilet. Fleetingly, he looked at his reflection in the mirror. With his reptilian look and shaved head, he can easily see his mug on an ex-convict's identification sheet. His face was chiseled in the way that those who spend more much time outdoors than indoors do. There was a blur in his expression, a mix of distress and resilience.

His succinct things rattled about in his backpack, filling it to the two-thirds: clothes, toiletries, and a metal cup. That was all he had, aside from his Lip watch from the seventies, his Swiss knife, and a few Euros.

He would stand at the sidewalk across the street to get a good look at the building. Recently renovated, it has been standing for at least two centuries. It was particularly narrow, lightly leaning between two juggernauts stopping a drunk from falling over. It had four floors with an attic and a slate roof where a zinc-framed œil-de-bœuf window was installed.

Each floor has a single apartment, and each apartment had one tenant. The all seemed to be single, solitary, and without children.

Beyond the main door, there were two opaque windows embellished with volutes in cast iron, four metal letter boxes that were lined against a wall of a humid corridor under a low vault. One could sprain an ankle against the historical pavement before stumbling into the courtyard. It was a somber bottleneck where primary colored recycling bins stood. The smell of rotting fish mingled with that of fermented fruits.

On his office door – and in his childhood years, it would have a window with an embroidered curtain that gently parted at each intrusion – the owner taped a laminated paper detailing the new caretaker's surname, given name, his starting date and his working hours. Yes, that was indeed him! The homeless guy now had a roof over his head; he felt like someone, for the first time in many years.

His new work started the following morning. He could spend his last day of vacation engaged in his usual activity: begging. He changed from his 'special appointment costume' into his all-around getup: jeans, polyester hooded sweater, rubber shoes, dark shades, and baseball cap. Thus he went into the small city of Puits-Magdelon, where the weekly market took place.

His name was Sylvain Wolf. Under his benign aspect, his name carries trials that he had endured since his childhood days – a bandage that never came off. As early as kindergarten, he suffered the first mockeries: *'Sylvain Wolf, where are you?'*, *'The Big Bad Sylvain Wolf'*... During recess, his classmates watched him for the joy of scampering, screaming 'Look out, here comes the wolf!' It had been game, of course, but one that holds much weight.

In elementary school, children's humor was enriched as the same time as their language. The daily repetition of their jokes was an ordeal: 'Hey, Wolf! Go to the dentist. He'll say, "Oh, such big teeth you have!" 'Or: "It smells weird. So, Big Bad Wolf, did you come with the three little pigs?' The college years brought on their finest, 'So did grandma taste good?' This was followed by impersonations of the libidinous Tex Avery Wolf. At 14 years old, a few boys in his class hung out at the corner of a street going, 'Hey, girls! Have you seen the wolf yet?' They then stooped to the ground and pulled his underwear down in front of a crowd of gawkers. Such humiliation was never forgiven, nor forgotten – never.

Sylvain got used to exclude himself to try to mitigate the pain of being a scapegoat – a vain attempt that doubled the agony.

His parents had an official showcase of jewelers, allowing them to engage in smuggling gold in the back room. They were totally monopolized by their business, spoke only of that, lived only for that. 'I have something else to do than to take care of the small ordinary miseries of a schoolboy,' said his mother before sending him out to play. They brought him neither support nor consolation, much less love. They ignored their only son and were content to store him away: 'He's a shy boy.

He keeps to himself.' This dismissive diagnosis, obscuring the causes of his isolation, immured Sylvain all the more. The pain of his parents' indifference weighed more in his heart than his classmates' mockery. Throughout his life, the adult wolf would bring the rejected child with him.

Envious neighbors discovered his parents' backdoor business and took a pleasure in reporting them to authorities. His father and mother were arrested and imprisoned. Sylvain was just 16 years old. He refused to visit them. Whether or not it was a painful choice, he chose never see them again. He just paid for their eventual burials, years later, without attending. His mother, suffering from appendicitis in prison, died in the hospital due to a nosocomial infection. As for his father, he made a failed attempt at escaping, followed by a successful suicide attempt: he had swallowed broken glass.

From the beginning of his parents' sentence, Sylvain had ended his schooling. He then enjoyed a brief respite from the taunts. It was however relayed by other troubles associated with gradual entry into a society keen on mocking him.

'Name?'

'Wolf.'

'W-o-l-f. Like a wolf?'

Sylvain no longer knew in what tone to answer – and it has been that case for a while. The issue fells on him with ridiculous regularly. It was water torture, each drop as heavy as lead. It was the straw that breaks the camel's back. Every time he tries to anticipate the reply, it was failure:

'My name was Wolf. Like a wolf.'

'Pardon? W-o-l-f-l-i-k ... and then?'

'W-o-l-f!'

'Ah! Wolf. Like a wolf?'

The refrain has nagged at for so long ... It went from the reduction in hysterics, resignation to rebellion, from the desire to slap up to the desire to kill. Of course, his name was not asked for every day. However, Sylvain Wolf has become what others have made him a shy and lonely soul. A wildling, some say. Villainous? No, but...

For over an hour he sat cross-legged on the floor, leaning against an empty flower box. He set his metal cup in front him, within which pennies have already stumbled in. Since it was market day, there was quite a level of noise in the hall and surrounding streets, where the small crowd flowed. Merchants and customers chatter, laugh openly or gently – it goes from guffaws to giggles – exchanging salaams and, of course, gossip. Gossip, with its vegetable name, handsomely feeds the good people.

The bells of the neighboring church stir the air with vibrating sounds that go above the human hubbub. Sylvain jumped. Already the end of the Mass! He rushed into the shortcut leading to the square. The passage was just enough to sneak in while hunching one's shoulders, between the foothills at the rear of the church's facade of the church and a black grimed gable. An overpowering smell of urine assaulted his nostrils and penetrated into his sinuses. Tears came to his eyes.

Regulars baptized the passage as: 'The cut-throat of Pissing Parishioner.'

Sylvain figured the funeral masses brought him less than wedding masses, but more than the usual Sundays, because the liturgy was a source of savings for those who make the rounds – throughout the year for the most industrious. If a Christian had the tendency to choose the spring and summer to get married, however, they choose no season to die. The informed beggar also knows that the charitable attitude has its variants. Coming off a wedding mass, the merry revelers, made guilty by the presence of the needy, are inclined to generosity. At the funeral, the reactions are different. There are those who really are heartbroken and, of those, there was nothing to hope for; but there were all the others, taken with superstitious jitters fueled by the omnipresence of death, just in case they perform a gesture towards their neighbor, as if they were buying an indulgence.

That morning, many came for the funeral for an old, well loved countrywoman. The coins jingled merrily in Sylvain's cup. The church square was empty. There were only a few stragglers dressed in dark, gathered in small lively groups. They certainly will not miss the great opportunity to chat. Most came for that, sometimes from far away, from the surrounding countryside. Sylvain moved away. He will buy bread, boar pâté and a beer; and the newspaper with its obituaries. He shook the key to the lodge in his hand, warm in his pocket. He cannot wait to have lunch, at home.

Over the three months that had passed, Sylvain had come across the tenants of the building several times – brief, civilized and cold contact. The exchanges were non-existent. Not even time to talk about the weather. He did not see them talking to each other. As of the present time, he knew them by face, save for the tenant on the first floor. It was a male. He did not know more. 'Edgar Huggins – 1st floor' was printed on the label of the regularly checked mailbox. If he could not hear him walking on the creaking parquet above his lodge, Sylvain would wonder if he existed. He never saw him. He often tried to spot a moving curtain, an open window, a silhouette or a hand that closed the accordion shutters. Nothing to do. The tenant kept its mystery, and Sylvain, his curiosity.

3:30 am. The whereabouts of Edgar Huggins made the floorboards whine and wake Sylvain.

There was movement on the landing.

A door, upon which someone held the latch, slid in slow motion, a lock was double-locked, and then muted sound of socks are heard on the stairs. This was it, Edgar Huggins came out of his home. Sylvain did not want to pass up the opportunity: he decided to follow him.

Somewhat agitated, quickly dressed, he watched the pfuitt of the automatic groom, followed by the clack of the building's door – familiar noises that punctuated his daily life for three months. As a precaution, he waited for a few seconds before going out in turn into the street. On his left, he saw a figure wearing a wide-brimmed hat and wearing a raincoat. The Incorruptible Style of 1930's Chicago. The approach was not that of an elderly man. Sylvain had masterminded a whole novel: an embittered old man, without family, was cloistered at home, did not open the door to anyone, fiercely resistant to his unique heirs (great nephews he barely knew), who threatened to send to a nursing home with the hope of speeding up his life's end... but it was not to be! The character was large, fine, with a stilted gait, back straight, head up; a shifting aristocratic morgue with the vaudeville character of one who came down the stairs in socks.

A damp fog blurred the orange light of lanterns perched high on the facades. It was the dead time of the night when the night owls have finished their day, while the early birds have not yet begun. They were just both in the streets. Sylvain had no hope of going unnoticed. He feigned nonchalance of one who had no reason to hide. Not easy to be clever when the heart's galloping like a racehorse against his chest.

The man took the direction of the industrial area. It was an avenue of skinny, shedding prune trees, where stood a row of tin sheds and other concrete warehouses – there were not even one or two dwellings. This did not reassure Sylvain. There was nothing in the area to justify his presence at such an hour. He gave up. The moment Sylvain changed his mind, the man pivoted and turned. He might have been aware of being followed, as it was intuitive to humans. With his hood folded over the head, hands clenched in his pockets, Sylvain inched away as quietly as possible. Above all, do not run. And if Edgar Huggins was going to follow him in turn? He took a peek behind him, then a second one more deliberate. The other was not there. Sylvain took off, running through the few remaining hundred meters.

Back in his office, he went bed dressed and took the time to calm down. Following a man without knowing why... what was it? What did he want to know?

Sylvain's contract stated sixty hours of work per month for the building's maintenance. In addition, he had the official accommodation provided to ensure his presence day and night. The owner heavily clarified that the main reason for hiring was: the tenants' safety, comfort, well-being and blah blah blah. With sixty hours paid at the hourly minimum wage, Sylvain did not sneer at that. A complement should not be overlooked, however small it may be.

This afternoon saw the funeral of the former mayor of Puits-Magdelon. It was something not to miss. There will be people: the random and the beautiful. Germain Languerrand was appreciated, even loved, by a large majority of Magdelonais. He caught 90% at each election. He was a monument 187cm of muscle and fat. He maintained his prominent belly in suspended pants hitched up high, closer to his armpits than his navel. A piece of his rumpled shirt stuck under the straps always slipped from his pants. Often dripping with sweat, he stripped his jacket, summer and winter, and curled his sleeves on his forearm. People shoved each other to greet him, sometimes for the sake of his handshake. He used both of his hands. With a look that made the insincere look pale, he then passed on his energy and love of life.

He defined himself as a nonconformist and a rebel. Germain made fun of everything. His position as mayor provided him opportunities to cram joke, one heavier than the next. At every wedding, the groom had no escape: 'Welcome to the cuckolds of Puits-Magdelon and its surroundings!' was the ceremonial introduction of the Mayor, wearing his venerable scarf. Delighted with his joke completely hackneyed, he added a quip for the uncomfortable bride, 'If you do not know what to do from 5 to 7, I am available to all my administered.' And to every child, he invariably said, 'Say hello to Daddy!' So Germain juggled with the clichés, without ever tiring his audience who craved for more.

He was a notorious unbeliever. He did not hesitate to boast of it, without worrying about losing votes among the parishioners. Besides, that was not the case, as he retained the same advantage in votes in each election. He addressed the priest, 'Hey, father! Better monitor your flock. I know the people who vote for me, as I am an unbeliever and a rake!' The priest, a childhood friend with a tolerant spirit would answer, 'Oh, my mayor! It was thanks to my prayers that the good Lord forgives you.'

Rabelaisian orgies ravaged insidiously beautiful Germain constitution. The one called 'our jovial Puits-Magdelon' began to weaken. His liver called uncle. Cirrhosis evolved into a cancer that gnawed on at high speed. It thrived at the same rate at which the man lived. He had to leave his town hall. Some wept administered.

It was agonizing when he told those around him: 'Wisdom was to make enough stupid to never reach the age of wisdom.' He died at the age of 41. The maxim remained famous in Puits-Magdelon. Now some Magdelonais do not know where it came from. Also they add sententiously: '... to paraphrase the philosopher.'

So, the good life has a short life. On the other hand, there were the living dead whose longevity made records as social protection taught them to forego the pleasures of life to make it last as long as possible.

Germain's religious burial was a flagrant offense in breaching the dead's will. It was a request from his older sister, Marie-Jeanne Languerrand, a pillar of the church. The bigot was known to spend hours kneeling on a straw kneeler, always the same, first in the central nave for two or three hours straight, every day. Eventually, she gave off smells of incense and melted candle. As soon as someone crossed her path, she made the face of a virgin and martyr. Virgin, no one doubted it. Martyrdom, no one knew. All who knew Germain heard some hearty words about her: 'There was only one ass-blessed per family. God chose that of my sister.'

Upon Germain's death, Marie-Jeanne Languerrand begged the priest to give a religious ceremony for her brother. The priest hesitated. He imagined her brother's wrath. His thunderous shouting matches reached him from beyond. Under pressure from many citizens, Christians or not, he relented.

Sylvain prepared for the big day of Germain Languerrand's funeral. At the town's annual fair, he bought a pair of pants, a jacket and shoes – seven Euros in all. There tossed them all in a plastic bag and changed in public toilets before arriving at the church, dressed in standard camouflage, taking away the risk of being recognized.

In brown corduroy, the jacket made him look more like a bourgeois on a weekend than a vagrant in need. However, the matching pants gave it a clownish appearance. Too short, it revealed his bare ankles and feet in box slumped moccasins. To top it off, a black and white Peruvian hat swallowed his eyebrows; a gray scarf covered his nose, sitting under dark glasses.

Arriving a little ahead of time, he set himself near the door of the church at the foot of three steps. The footsteps of millions of believers have weathered them, digging in an uninterrupted cycle over the centuries. From generation to generation, they sent their faith, their hope to be forgiven for their sins and their fear of hell.

Sylvain believed in nothing. Sin? No. Forgiveness? Even less. Hell? The evidence he needed was all on earth. So, why invent something a beyond imagination? No need to add more.

As expected, there were so many people that many were standing shoulder to shoulder against the aisles and narthex. Sylvain saw them through the door remained that remained open despite the cold. A wave of motion in the crowd pressed to the end indicated that the mass has started. Bells rang gloomily, accompanying the march of undertakers. A coffin covered with the tricolor flag was crammed into the hearse while Magdelonais scattered on the square. The small coins start to click in Sylvain's metal cup when suddenly a 50 Euro note was delicately placed by a hand gloved of a fine caramel colored goatskin.

It was something never seen in Sylvain's life!

He was so absorbed in contemplating the note, when he looked up to see the donor, it was too late. The man already had his back turned. He walked away with measured steps as if he was saving his energy. He wore an incorruptible raincoat and a Borsalino hat. Sylvain obviously recognized this approach and this outfit: the tenant of the first floor.

Sylvain will follow, once more. He still did not know why. It was irresistible. If the other saw him, it can always be justified: he wanted to thank him for the bill.

A new chase began. He hoped that it does not end once again in the industrial area – but no. Edgar Huggins goes into the suburbs of the Lower Town and borrowed an avenue of naked and mutilated lime trees, stumps outstretched to heaven. The slap of the November wind was scathing. The people of Puits-Magdelon are in the cemetery, the suburbs are deserted, and Sylvain's presence was far from discrete.

Edgar Huggins stopped at a disused pub. On the facade, above a metal curtain, a chipped sign painted in bottle green had turned into almond green in the bad weather. One could still read a faded inscription: *Au Bon Bouilleur*. Edgar Huggins was bent for a long time on the locks on the door, then disappeared inside the room, without looking back.

Sylvain was crestfallen on the opposite sidewalk, dancing from one foot to the other. His feet naked and cold, he stomped about for several minutes, then left empty-handed.

Over the following weeks, Sylvain had not heard Edgar Huggins leaving home, day or night. He did not encounter him in the building or elsewhere. Yet he had gone to all sorts of masses, despite the biting cold.

As soon as he heard the creaking parquet on the first floor, he climbed on his kitchen table and glued his ear to the ceiling, on the lookout for a clue. He did not even know what he hoped to hear. At night he doubled his attention, ready to spring to follow. He was so tense that his insomnia became chronic. He became comatose. His brain seemed disconnected from his exhausted body, which he fought as much as he can. During the day, Sylvain fell asleep without realizing it, a quick nap, at any time, in increments of minutes. He was convinced that the other upstairs took advantage of these sudden deaths to escape gently.

Sylvain returned repeatedly to the bistro *Au Bon Bouilleur* at the outskirts of town, hours spying around. He did not notice any up-and-coming suspect. Nothing. He even went prowling in the industrial area, where he had abandoned his first chase. Sylvain's obsession consumed him. He lost his senses. He suffered a severe form of attachment to the tenant of the first floor.

The first time he met Josée Nadar, it was on the second floor landing. Sylvain was sweeping the terracotta tiles, when he heard footsteps slip into the apartment – stopping, not shuffling. He felt watched by the eyepiece. The door opened, releasing a nauseating smell of burnt fat. There walked a fat woman in a blouse of purple and pink flowers, the likes of which were sold by the dozen in the markets of France.

'Must you be the new caretaker?' She asked, no pretenses.

'Yes, ma'am.'

'What's your name?'

'Sylvain Wolf.'

There was a brief silence; short, but enough to make Sylvain seethe internally. 'Wolf. Like a wolf. She'll say it, I know she'll say it!'

'That's one beautiful name.' she murmured simply.

Sylvain concentrated on his broom to hide his puzzlement. Josée Nadar had a request.

'Well, Mr. Wolf, would you be willing to bring me my mail to my home, to spare me the stairs? My poor legs, you understand. Phlebitis. I can die from it, you see.' she said, holding out a leg Sylvain.

In fact, that poor leg was a post without ankle held in dark brown support stockings. Sylvain could refuse nothing to the lady who had just told him he had a beautiful name. He accepted without a second thought – without hurry either. There was soon a second request:

'Maybe you could do some shopping for me from time to time?'

That was already more restrictive. However, Sylvain felt obliged to acquiesce. He had no idea what was in store for him with this seemingly harmless Josée Nadar.

He became trapped upon the first step. Josée Nadar pitched him her shopping list and gave him a 10 Euro note. The amount exceeded the triple. Traders did not do credit, and Sylvain had to advance the money. When he presented the bills, Josée Nadar spat out her lungs. 'Thief!' She yelled, theatrically, in the stairwell. Not a single tenant appeared. Sylvain gave up on getting a refund.

The following week, she casually handed him her list. Sylvain refused, friendly, but determined. Josée Nadar flashed him a look. She prepared a cocktail of venom, the strong venom of an effervescent tablet.

Thus he received, two days later, a letter from the owner of the building:

Sir,

The tenant of the second floor, Josée Nadar, has just informed me of events which, I hope, will not happen again.

It seems that you refused to render her small services (bringing up her mail, shopping, etc.). I am very unpleasantly surprised by your behavior.

I remind you that it was stated in your contract that you must be fully 'available' for tenants.

You are therefore required to facilitate the life of this elderly and sickly woman.

In addition, Ms. Nadar complained of altercations between you and her, about money that you have tried to steal it (by not give her back her shopping money, for example).

My letter was a warning. If I have knowledge like incidents, I will not hesitate to break the contract between us.

I give you one last chance.

Cordially,

Bérengère Salvignol

Sylvain understood immediately that it he was stuck in a hopeless case. In the absence of evidence, the owner was ready to decide in favor of the tenant, without finding out who was doing what and who was right. He resigned to himself.

That day, he saw no way out of this spiral of fraud and blackmail. Spending on Josée Nadar weighed too heavy on his budget. With the support of the owner, she allowed him to fund all of her food shopping.

Either he complied, or he can say goodbye to his lodgings and to his pay.

The city center was closed vehicles on market days. Goods stood stall to stall against the narrow streets that exclusively offer their space to pedestrians. They took the opportunity to cause pedestrian traffic. People are surprised by sudden stops, anywhere, preferably in the middle of the road, Here and there, forming small indivisible crowds.

Sylvain has had to overcome several before arriving in the hall.

He stood in line to the butcher-delicatessen. The craftsman was paunchy, wrapped in a bleached apron. With gleaming cheekbones, a joke in his lips, his image completely matched with the jovial clichés of his profession. Customers appreciated the character, which made them easier to swallow its expensive products.

Sylvain's shortened nights failed him, he was numb and absent. An opportunist took the chance to take his turn in the queue. He let them.

'Hey, hey, Mr Wolf,' the butcher called out.

Head back, eyes closed, lips forward, he began a lousy imitation of a howling wolf.

'The queue's on you-ou-ou-ou, Mr Wolf, woof woof!'

He winked knowingly to his customers who grinned stupidly, as do a captured public. Sylvain did not flinch. He held out Josée Nadar's shopping list to the merchant, who suddenly darkened. Silently, the man cut slices of pâté, rosette, garlic sausage and ham on the bone. He added two jars of duck confit, and wrapped them all up. Sylvain paid.

The look of the butcher was benevolent.

'Goodbye, Mr. Wolf. No hard feelings, right?'

Sylvain thanked and continued to go around. Without a word, he handed Josée Nadar's list to different traders. Week after week, they have become accustomed to it. They know who Wolf was, and Sylvain was welcomed with kindness, even if it felt suspicious. Sylvain was worried that it was pity. As if everyone already knew his story.

The town of Puits-Magdelon had about 7500 inhabitants. People knew what their neighbors were up to, even before the neighbor knew. And when they did not know, they did not trouble for so little: they guessed, they assumed, they invented.

Sylvain limply went back to Rue du Vau-L'Eau, a basket in each hand. There was a disheveled fury, trying to knock on the door of his lodge. Nadar put in all her strength, both fists simultaneously, while shouting: 'Open, Mr Wolf. I know you're there!' As soon as she saw him, she rushed to him, her poor legs curiously lively that morning.

'Where have you been?'

She foamed. Her shrill voice contrasted with Sylvain's drawling.

'At the market, doing your shopping.'

'Then take them home!' She ordered eyeing the baskets.

Sylvain went up the stairs behind the fury. She stopped screaming, too breathless to shout any longer. He heard her grumble between two nasty coughs. 'Con man, bastard, junk, scum.'

Upon reaching the landing, she eagerly seized the bag, then slammed the door of her apartment. While the jamb shook, she barked, 'Go away!'

Sylvain was silent. For how many years has he kept quiet?

The postman waited at the bottom of the stairs with a parcel for Odon Gadelorge, the third floor tenant.

'Leave it to me, I'll do it.' He said to the postman who seemed happy to gain a few extra minutes on his round.

Odon Gadelorge opens the door, shirtless in overalls whose original blue color disappeared under paint stains.

Frail shoulders, protruding collarbones, stunted arms, with wrinkled neck like that of a chicken. Odon Gadelorge had a sickly appearance. A helmet hair dyed coal black emphasized the ash gray color of his skin. Two strands sweep over his eyes and very close to his nose, ringed with purple. With his eyebrows questioning, the man looked uninviting for someone who does not like to be disturbed.

Through the open door, Sylvain saw a smoke shop also serving as an artist workshop. A long trestle table, cluttered with brushes held hairs into the air in glass jars, occupied a third of the living space. Many canvases placed on easels or on the ground were portraits. Tobacco pipe fragrances, thinners, linseed oil and paint created an unusual atmosphere, one that Sylvain would like to explore. He was not invited in. Odon Gadelorge thanked him for the parcel, obviously in a hurry to finish with the intruder.

Despite the less than lukewarm welcome, Sylvain said it would be wise to gradually get to know this tenant. Perhaps he knew who Edgar Huggins was.

18:28. The tenant on the fourth floor will be there soon. Maryse Beurdelet had a working person's regular schedule, someone very, very punctual. 8:30 in the morning and 6:30 at night, five days a week.

She was no longer young, but she has never been. She was not old either. When she gets older, it was barely noticeable. Her manner of dress, her hair, her walk, her greeting, unsmiling... everything exudes boredom. She was smooth, she was beige. He found it distressing. She wore a large mouse gray coat with a round neck, buttoned up, concealing a body that Sylvain has never even glimpsed, aside from thin calves in opaque tights and narrow feet in flat shoes. Medium size, medium stature, she was an average woman in medium. She smelled of lavender soap and fabric softener. A woman like that could never smell of sweat.

Sylvain made up a movie: Maryse Beurdelet all legs in the air. Ah! It should be seen more closely.

Fritch, fritch, went the vigorous scrubbing brush strokes Sylvain gave on the pavement of the corridor, resonating in the vault. He had not heard Maryse Beurdelet enter. Caught in between dirty thoughts, he blushed instantly. She sneaked, ass pinched tightly between soapy puddles.

Stammering Sylvain, who was better off silent.

'Good evening, Miss Beurdelet. Watch out, uh... it's slippery.'

In response, the girl gave him a discreet nod, her troubadour hair barely moving.

The start of a regular early evening at No. 9 Rue du Vau-L'Eau.

On the fourth floor, Maryse Beurdelet, naked in her bathroom, groomed herself carefully. In the third, Odon Gadelorge painted portraits. In the second, Josée Nadar cooked up dishes with supplies purchased by Sylvain. In the first, Edgar Huggins played the invisible tenant. On the ground floor, Sylvain Wolf was about to face hours of insomnia.

CHAPTER 2

It had to happen. Marie-Jeanne Languerrand, sister of the late mayor, addressed Sylvain on Christmas night, right out of the midnight mass.

In the wild, the frog and the tick have nothing in common. But within the Catholic Church, the benevolent frog and sanctimonious bug belong to the same species. Their Main Features: help others, even when they did not want to be helped.

Thus Marie-Jeanne Languerrand insisted that Sylvain come meet her the next day at the Catholic Relief Services. This was to inform humanitarian aid and it can benefit Puits-Magdelon. And thus she meowed with a slimy honeyed voice.

'You cannot stay out in the cold. Do you have a place to sleep?'

Sylvain failed to respond. He put his empty cup under his jacket and walked away, discouraged. Not only it made him miss one of the best recipes of the year, but in addition he was spotted.

The frog-tick being stubborn, he assumed that she would never let go. He must now give up begging at the church of Puits-Magdelon. What a mess.

A white envelope was slipped under the door waiting for him on the floor of his office. Sylvain walked on returning from the first market of the New Year. He fixed his eyes on the paper rectangle. 'MISTER S. WOLF' was carefully written in capital letters. He did not want to touch this letter, and he did not even to pick it up; it was inevitably a letter from the owner.

'That's it. I'm screwed. I'm fired. What's Nadar done this time? What's that crazy-ass woman want?' Sylvain felt rage tense his jaws.

'She'll see what my name is, that old bat!' He continued to rant. When he added 'My name was Wolf, like a wolf!' It was better to stir up hatred.

With his back to the wall, he slid down slowly to a squat. By looking more closely at the letters written in dark blue ink, a detail caught his eye: it was written in fountain pen, a rare practice in the 21st century.

And if it was Edgar Huggins? Yes, it would be like him.

The idea came, and took shape. His movements were nervous when he unsealed the envelope. Inside, two notes of fifty Euros and a business card with embossed characters:

Edgar Huggins
Honorary Mayor

Below, letters were finely drawn in pen: 'Best wishes. EH' At the bottom right was the street address of Rue du Vau-L'Eau. No telephone number.

Sylvain nervously flipped the card between his index and middle finger. It was an excuse to go to the unknown tenant. Up to the first floor, ring the bell, 'I wanted to thank you...' No, he will first go to the public library to check the dictionary.

'Honorary Mayor ...? What's an honorary mayor?'

Winter was just beginning. Cold already settled in for several weeks, and was intensifying. The sidewalks were treacherous. He dragged brownish sleet hiding patches of ice. Temperatures veered below zero, the lower layers of clouds burst in icing rain. Sylvain had the wind in his back. Gusts propelled him forward, rain dripping down his black coat, wetting his pantlegs.

Upon entering the library, he came upon the face of an idle woman happy to receive his visit. She worked very hard to keep him in for as long as possible. First, she talked about the especially harsh winter this year. There, it was done. Then, to prolong her pleasure she showed him the arrangement of shelves and grading structures. It was done. Running out of ideas, she signaled to Sylvain that she was at his disposal – with an insistent and hopeful look – to help him choose; if he so desired, of course.

Sylvain, unaccustomed to such solicitude, seized the opportunity.

'I just came to look at the dictionary. An honorary mayor ... you know what that is?

'Yes I do. He was a former mayor, who no longer has any function. The title was purely honorary. I think he must have worked for many years to qualify for this title.'

'How many years?'

'Ah! I'll get the dictionary!' she replied, clearly delighted to have work to do.

She unfolded her seat with both hands readjusting her restrictive narrow skirt. As soon as her back was turned, he looked to her shapely behind. She must have been suspecting it, as she seemed to be swaying her hips.

When she returned, Sylvain noted that she had fixed her hair and removed her jacket. She arched her back to push her generous bosoms forward, molded in a turtleneck sweater. Since the breasts in question seem to have a good fifty years, Sylvain thought that they stood quite well. She brought under her arm an encyclopedia volume, and took on a virtuous air.

A few pages later, she read aloud: *The title of honorary mayor: 18 years of service required. Responsibilities carried out in municipal functions (as deputy, advisor) are taken into account.*

Sylvain released the burning question.

'You know a certain Edgar Huggins?'

'An Anglo-Saxon writer?'

'No. Honorary Mayor of Puits-Magdelon'

'Oh no! If he had been mayor for years, I wouldn't have missed it! I was born in Puits-Magdelon, and always have lived. My family has been here for three generations.'

On a pithy 'Thanks for everything' Sylvain prepared to leave. The frustrated librarian moved her pawn.

'I hope to see you again soon.'

'Yes. Goodbye.'

Why not, he thought furtively.

She would not let go.

'My name was Guylaine Monteil. And you?'

'Sylvain Wolf.'

'Wolf? Like a wolf?'

Sylvain shrugged. He no longer wanted to see her again.

Alone again in her library, Guylaine Monteil bit her lower lip.

Back in his lodgings, he stumbled on two shopping bags waiting for him. They were full of provisions for the lonely old woman who ate like a large family. With all that, he had almost forgotten. It was urgent to deliver Josée Nadar groceries, before she shows off in her spectacular role as the victim.

As usual, she did not open the door, and left it ajar, just enough so that he could pass her the baskets one by one.

What was going on in her head? Sylvain held out his arm, and gave a powerful thrust against Josée Nadar's chest and managed to effortlessly walk backwards into the apartment. He entered in turn to close the door with a kick, and firmly shook Nadar with one arm turned into noose around his neck. Everything happened so fast. She was too stunned to react. Sylvain covered Nadar's gaping mouth, who threatened to scream. For once! He held her back against his torso. She was lifted from the ground. Then he dragged her to the bed, threw her on it, pinning her to the mattress. He straddled Nadar's belly, rolling her eyes comically.

'I'm not here to rape you. Don't hope for it. Just here kill you,' said Wolf, in an ironic tone.

With all his weight, he pressed against that hated face, that voracious pie hole. It was there where he wanted to make her suffer. First, cut out her tongue and shove it down her neck, down her throat. May Nadar forever hold her peace! Then he would tear at the corners of her mouth, file her teeth tear them out, pour salt – no, rather acid – on her raw gums. The famous scenes of torture in the history of mankind rolled through Sylvain Wolf's confused mind. He felt harassed by those pent-up thoughts. But no, he will not do any of that. He will kill her by smothering her under a pillow. That was it – a perfect death for a perfect crime.

The agony was endless, and the victim was tough. Healthy, well-fed, Sylvain noted.

Two fingers on the carotid artery. No pulse. Josée Nadar was dead.

Now he had to wrestle with the body to remove her quilted dressing gown; an ordeal in itself. Then he positioned the remains in heavy flannel discolored nightgown on the bed. The melee made him nauseous. It was not over. The dead needed to be positioned: lying on the right side, and slightly bent knees raised, left hand on the thigh – the image of a peacefully sleeping woman.

Following setup: pull the sheets and blanket in a bunch up to the nose, place the robe folded on the chair in the room and quietly line up the stuffed wool slippers at the foot of the bed.

Finishing touches: leave on the kitchen table baskets filled with provisions, shopping list, and even a few coins to simulate – such a good idea – a duly issued change.

Before leaving, check that there was no suspicious disorder at the entrance. Finally, head down the stairs without particular care: he just went to deliver Nadar her groceries, just like every week.

Once in the refugee of his lodgings, Sylvain let out a long sigh, like punctured tire.

On the floor below, Edgar Huggins heard it all, Sylvain knew it. How could it be otherwise? The buildin's soundproofing was just as good as cardboard. His bursting into Nadar's was brutal, oak flooring had to have creaked loudly. Nothing says Edgar Huggins was present at the time, though, Sylvain failed to budge. Huggins was the main auditory witness, and he will be questioned by investigators first off, should there be any investigation.

Sylvain looked at the two crisp new banknotes of fifty Euros. What was behind Edgar Huggins' excessive generosity? If this gentleman was rich, why did he live in a modest two-room flat in Rue Vau-L'Eau in Puits-Magdelon? In any case, the money was for Sylvain. Just for him from now on. His head tilted against the back of the couch. He fell asleep for hours on end.

Suddenly awakened, Sylvain caught a bad cold and broke into hot sweating. The knock on the door were vigorous. It must be the fists of a cop. Already? In that was case, it was better to prepare an innocent air. And just how was an innocent air?, he asked himself. A poker face will do.

Sylvain opened the damn door that did not even have an eyehole. No cops in sight, only the impatient postman, arms full with a package for Odon Gadelorge.

'I'm in a hurry. No time to go up to the third floor. I'll leave the parcel?'

'Of course!'

The postman has never seen the caretaker of No. 9 so eager and smiling.

Sylvain was happy to have an opportunity to go back to Odon Gadelorge. Often there were packets for him. It seems that he ordered his painting materials in a specialty store in Paris. The tenant was at home. Following the first bell, he appeared, surrounded by clouds of smoke – the aroma of diluted tobacco, soaring high upon an ether known only to himself, he took time to step out on the landing:

'What does Mr. Wolf want?'

'A package for you.'

'Come in,' he said to Sylvain who had been waiting for it.

Odon Gadelorge motioned for him to put the package in the kitchen, the only place in the apartment where a few square centimeters were available. Then he opened a bottle of absinthe and filled two tacky glasses.

The silent men toast. Bottoms up. Other round. There! The two knew how to communicate without words. The third round somewhat loosened their tongues.

'Do you only paint portraits?'

'Yes.'

'People you know?'

'Know, dear Sir, that the painter is a soul hoarder. He knows his model as he painted. He makes them his own, he penetrates far as he was penetrated. Do you understand?'

'Mmm...'

The exchanges were completed for today. Odon and Sylvain separate. Until next delivery.

Passing on the second floor landing, Sylvain had a brief vision of Nadar rotting as the days went by along her deli and vegetables. Having reached the ground floor, he arrived in time to see someone melt into the courtyard's darkness. Edgar Huggins! No, he did not dare to call out to him. Not yet. So he followed.

With a sudden return to his lodgings, he pulled on his jacket, hat, and scarf. Sylvain got mad, lost time. Once outside, he looked with his own eyes the silhouette of the man he knew. He saw him turn the corner of the Rue du Vau-L'Eau and Rue La Pitauderie.

At the end of that January day that already mingled with dusk, the people of Puits-Magdelon, stiff with cold, walked like puppets with jammed joints. With three glasses of absinthe, Sylvain had stored calories. That was good.

Edgar Huggins took to the lead outskirts of the Ville Basse until the *Bon Bouilleur*.

Sylvain kept a little distance on the other side of the icy road, behind the trunk of a lime tree.

'Mr. Wolf!'

The tone of voice was not threatening, but it was rather comely. The prompt was polite and respectful. The surprise halted Sylvain.

'Mr Wolf,' Edgar Huggins said again. 'Come, please!'

As if a little boy, Sylvain came out of his ridiculous hiding place. He went to join Edgar Huggins while avoiding slipping on the ice, and that took him some time. Hiding his agitated state when they shook hands was not easy either.

'Let's get inside,' whispered Huggins.

He gave way so as Sylvain can enter the disused pub. It was completely dark. Huggins lit a lighter and a gas lamp.

What supernatural phenomenon froze the places in time as if they were in the first half of the twentieth century? Furniture and equipment, nothing was missing. The air vibrated with the revelry and drinking songs memorized by the walls; it spread among the advertising posters, works of art dating from the years when they were en vogue – including along the dark tunnels of the Paris metro -- the benefits of alcohol, while the French RTM encouraged smokers to discover cigarettes. 'All done!' it said, the better to lure buyers.

Edgar Huggins invited Sylvain to sit at one of the tables of the haunted room.

'Whiskey?'

Sylvain did not respond. He saw himself as a fool that fell into the trap that he laid out himself.

They were face to face. Finally he beheld the cause of his insomnia! He actually looked like an object of insomnia. The man impresses with his anachronistic attire of cop or gangster. The edges of his hat were primed through years of research, his face partly camouflage by the dimly lit gas lamp, which had a spectral appearance in keeping with the decor. Sylvain distinguished an aquiline nose and a disdainful pout. He gave off enigmatic air as he smiled to himself when he tasted his whiskey through mannered sips. He was infatuated and detached.

'I followed you to thank you' ... starts Sylvain, mediocre.

Edgar Huggins, with a wave of his hand, signalled him to be quiet. He then pointed his black eyes upon those of Sylvain, who felt increasingly stupefied.

'I know everything, Mr. Wolf. I know you come from the street. I know how much you earn now. I know you are still begging. About the nosy Marie-Jeanne Languerrand, who spotted you, it seems. A kind soul, right? If she recognizes you, she will be keen to talk to our owner. You would be fired on the spot. What-will-people-say, you know. Not to mention tenant safety! A former homeless beggar: is he a man of trust? Questioned our own dear Bérengère, I know her so well! Me too, I could tell her about your little secret. Is that right, Mr. Wolf? Finally, I know you were victim of a plot by Josée Nadar, who plundered your meager income while insulting you. It wasn't a reason to kill her, wasn't it, Mr Wolf?

Sylvain was caught off guard. His answer clashed as badly as his replica of a bad actor.

'I don't know what you're talking about.'

'But of course you know! You can imagine that I heard everything. After your altercation, I saw you down the stairs, through the peephole in my door. I climbed to the second floor. Yes, Sir, I have the keys of Josée Nadar. Congratulations for your setup! But I doubt that the police would be fooled. Moreover, as a witness, I will work to put them on the right track. Your murder will be confirmed at autopsy. The media will dive into melodrama: the heinous crime against an elderly woman, doubtless a victim of sexual abuse – the overwhelming detail. Moreover, this was an isolated widow with no children, weakened by a serious illness... The jurors will not forgive, they are ruthless. You will be in in prison for bunch of years. Another version: I have not heard anything. Josée Nadar died in her sleep – Phlebitis, pulmonary embolism. It would be credible to the constabulary of Puits-Magdelon, which has other fish to fry. Isn't that right, Mr. Wolf?'

Sylvain found him sharp with his, 'Isn't that right, Mr. Wolf?'

'What do you want?'

'Ah! I see that you are reasonable. We can get along. I need a delivery boy.'

'A delivery boy? A delivery boy for what?'

'A delivery boy knowing delivery must know how to deliver without knowing what he's delivering.'

He paused, cleared his throat, just to check the effect of his poor joke. Sylvain did not get up. Huggins filled the glasses up to two thirds.

'The first deliveries will begin shortly. Oh, I forgot! From this day you stop following me. And I no longer want to see you wandering in the industrial area or keep watch near the *Bon Bouilleur*. That game is over. If you persist, I will have you removed. Your disappearance would not even be news: you already are an abandoned life. Is that right, Mr. Wolf? Have I made myself clear?'

Sylvain had not eaten anything since morning. The mixture of absinthe and whiskey made him dizzy. It was hard to follow a verbose individual. Little aware of the scandalous situation in which he was in up to his eyeballs, he asked, as it were a question of priority:

'The fifty Euro bills you gave me twice, why?'

'Bait, my dear man. Bait for the wolf from the wood. He he! Two bills like that, and there's more where they came from.'

'How much?'

'Hold your horses! We're not there yet. You must first prove yourself.'

'And if I refuse?'

'I turn you in for the murder of Josée Nadar. You are free to go get fucked for years by fellow inmates who don't use any lube. Is that right, Mr. Wolf?'

Sylvain was stuck. It felt wrong.

'One last thing,' said Huggins. 'I remain as the gentleman of the first floor, with whom you have no contact. We never had this interview, of course. You can say that I pay you to keep quiet until the end of your days. If by chance you get arrested, if by chance you speak, know this: what I have in store for you is worse than death. Others before you have begged for me to end them. Starting today, you belong to me, you will never escape me. Wherever you are, Mr. Wolf. In France, abroad or at the bottom of a prison cell. I am a powerful man, my network of relationships is vast. Get that into your thick skull. Now, go home. We will do nothing until the Nadar case is resolved. Up to you to take care of it first. Do not, under any circumstances, try to contact me. I'll be the one to contact you.

Sylvain rose and fell back again heavily in his chair. At the third attempt, he finally managed to stand. As he zigzagged, Edgar Huggins grabbed an arm and managed to head out with him.

Two steps away, a geyser of vomit gushed from his mouth and crashed like a puree on the frozen sidewalk. That was better. Sylvain returned home, his mind as empty as his stomach.

———————∾———————

'Hello, Miss Salvignol? It's Sylvain Wolf.'

'Yes?'

'I've called you to...'

'Be quick, Mr Wolf. I'm shockingly late.'

'I wanted to tell you, I haven't seen Ms. Nadar for several days. In itself, this isn't surprising, it happens often. But in general, she doesn't forget market day. So when I saw that she didn't give me her shopping list, I thought ...'

'Confound it, Mr. Wolf! I can't believe my ears! What are you waiting for to go ring at her door?'

'Done. She doesn't answer.'

'How long have you not seen her, you say?'

'A week.'

'Wait a minute. I'm looking for her phone number.'

The voice of Salvignol up a notch in exasperation.

'Goodness! Ms. Nadar has no telephone! I'll go see her.' She sighed, hanging up.

That was it, the first step. Call the owner in the presence of a witness.

'Thanks for the phone, Mr. Gadelorge.'

'As payment, go get us the bottle of absinthe in the kitchen. We'll finish together.'

Since his last drink, Sylvain avoided exceeding certain limits. Alcohol has left holes in his memory – more reason to be worried. He forgot many parts of his interview with Huggins. Among the shadows, there was one who works. He understood that Edgar Huggins made him sing. But since when did a blackmailer he proposed a salary?

The question remained, but that did not stop him from drinking with the artist.

Both men continue their polite conversation with 'Mr. Gadelorge' and 'Mr. Wolf.' For Sylvain, Odon Gadelorge was not only a man whose company he enjoyed. He liked him, and Gadelorge returned the sentiment..

'Would you give me your permission to paint your portrait?' timidly asked Gadelorge.

'Uh ...'

'Your face is poignant, Mr Wolf. I can no longer resist the attraction it exerts on the painter that resonates in me. I am magnetized. Do you understand? Each of your looks challenges me. Ah! What mix of pigments could I invent to paint the black of your eyes? Only my art could unveil the untold suffering you bury. Only my art can express this subtly and with the greatest respect your interiority. You are the model I have been looking for, for so long!'

The fancy speech disconcerted Sylvain.

'Please accept.' implored Gadelorge.

'I... how to say?'

'Thirty Euros for a two-hour session! You'll be paid at the end of each session.'

Sylvain was uncomfortable. Suddenly, he did not want money to come between him and his only buddy. But supplementing his income would not be refused. Despite Nadar's death his budget was a mess. As for Edgar Huggins' futuristic proposals, he waited to find out more.

'Mr Wolf? Is it yes?'

'Yes.'

Odon Gadelorge discreetly hid his joy. He walked towards Sylvain with an approach that strove to be solemn, which was not obvious with his skinny short legs, naked under a jumpsuit full of holes and stains of all colors. He put his hands on Sylvain's shoulders standing above him by fifteen centimeters. When Sylvain expected a new surge in the eyes of the painter that seemed to see through centuries, Odon Gadelorge only said, 'My friend.' Sylvain was only too touched to answer.

It had been nearly a week since his phone call to Bérengère Salvignol. The owner was not too worried.

Snug under the covers for two weeks, the body of the Nadar must be a feast for bacteria.

Sylvain was cleaning out the garbage in the yard. His hands numb from the cold took on mottled purplish tones.

18:31. In came, in order of appearance, Maryse Beurdelet (she was therefore a minute behind her usual arrival time) followed by Bérengère Salvignol. The two women were silent upon seeing Sylvain. He almost heard the sound of the voice of Maryse Beurdelet, but he still missed it.

While the latter concealed her embarrassment in her mailbox, the owner asked Sylvain.

'Have you heard from Ms. Nadar?'

'No, Miss. I ring the doorbell regularly. She no longer opens up.'

'Good. I'm heading up. I took my spare key.'

'They both take the stairs. Sylvain was dedicated to his trash with meticulousness multiplied by a hundred, while tending straining his ear as if to tear his eardrums. As expected, he did not take long to hear the shrill screams of women terrified by a horrifying vision. Yes, it was clear that the vision in question should not be appetizing. 'Go, valiant caretaker, fly to the rescue of these gentle ladies,' crooned Sylvain, hushed. He climbed the stairs in haste as loudly as possible to show his eagerness.

'Miss Salvignol? Do you need me?'

No answer. Beurdelet and Salvignol were there, frozen in the same way, a hand over their noses, eyes wide and staring at the bed where the remains of Nadar decomposed.

They raised the sheet, revealing the remains. The heated atmosphere of the small apartment amplified the stench of rot. Mixed with the musky scent of Salvignol was an additional infection. Sylvain was hypnotized against the proliferation of insects supposed to be hibernating at this time of the year. Green flies, lured by the smell came out of their lethargy. They laid eggs in every orifice, from the pores of the skin to the sphincters through the nostrils, ears, mouth. Whitish maggots -- oh the gluttons! – swarming. Nadar's ashen face was in tatters. It was difficult to recognize Nadar's anonymous dead head bristling with white hair. The larvae implanted in her body have fed handsomely. In two weeks, the first arrivals had time to reach adulthood. Squads of scavengers hum. Their flight was heavy and messy. They commuted between the bedroom and the kitchen spoiled pies adding their rotting acids to the pestilence.

Repulsed but fascinated, the man was hungry for horror shows. The woman as well, observed Sylvain.

'Come, ladies, get away from there.'

They follow him to the landing, dazed.

It was Maryse Beurdelet who spoke.

'Come with me, Miss Salvignol. It would be best for us to call.'

It was not the cutesy voice he had imagined. This was a serious voice, a bit broken though not much so, a voice that could almost make Beurdelet attractive. 'She's all cute and cuddly, this little lady,' said Sylvain disconnected this drama.

The owner locked the dead's apartment and followed Maryse Beurdelet. Sylvain looked at the two pairs of calves up the steps. He had never noticed that those of Maryse Beurdelet were so muscular.

At the fourth floor, the Salvignol spoke curtly.

'Mr Wolf, wait for me here. I have something to tell you.'

Two gendarmes showed up, accompanied by a young man with a brief case, probably the doctor on duty. Although he was beginner, it should not be too difficult to find death. One of the gendarmes and the doctor went upstairs, where they found the owner.

The other policeman remained with Sylvain in front of the office. He was a stocky strapped sausage in his uniform. He seemed very imbued with authority. He was solid, stuck upon his legs at shoulder-width apart. Then he went on the attack, arms folded, frowning eyebrows and mouth

'When did you last see Mrs. Josée Nadar?'

'Two weeks ago. It was a Tuesday, the market day.'

'Oh! And you waited two weeks to move?'

'No, I warned the owner after eight days. I called her up.'

Officers' footsteps stomped on the stairs. A colleague, a military training kind of fellow, descended.

The two gendarmes isolated themselves in the courtyard to discuss. They headed up the stairs together in sport. They stopped at the first floor; and rang the doorbell. All the agitation!

Edgar Huggins welcomed them. 'Gentlemen? What can I do for you?' Sylvain well recognized that voice well, one that evoked class. Huggins had the police enter his home. Sylvain, feinted, heard nothing.

The ballet continued. The doctor and the owner came down while the police went up. After Huggins, they visited Odon Gadelorge on the third floor, and then Maryse Beurdelet on the fourth. When they were finally all gathered downstairs Sylvain invited no one to get warm in his lodgings. The doctor made his exit – that made one; followed by the gendarmes, and there went two.

'You will be summoned to the police soon, Miss Salvignol. You, too, Mr. Wolf.' announced the stocky policeman in a military manner.

Sylvain remained in head-to-head with the owner. Her menacing scowl intrigued her. He noticed that she had a moon face, round eyes and mouth wedged between two fat cheeks. The cold flushed her nose, and she shivered. If she wanted to impress, she did it badly.

By detaching the syllables, she articulated

'You did not call me after eight days, Mr. Wolf. You called me that evening around 6 p.m., and I came im-me-di-ate-ly. Is that clear?'

A tic tugged at her upper lip at regular intervals. She was afraid, it showed, and Sylvain knew why. She could be accused of failing to assist a person in danger. It was not for nothing that he had provided a witness to make itself immune to this kind of accusation. The penalties were severe: imprisonment and hefty fine.

'The phone call, I already talked to the policeman who questioned me.' said Sylvain, feigning innocence.

Anger did not make Salvignol pretty.

'Listen to me, Mr. Wolf! You may say that you lied. You intended to warn me, but eventually...'

From a slightly mocking tone, Sylvain interrupted and added a layer.

'I used Mr. Gadelorge's phone to call you. He is a witness.'

'Really? This was not what Mr. Gadelorge said!'

Sylvain was silent. He could barely hear Salvignol's last words of. They came to him, distant, muffled by the fog that invaded his brain.

'Keep employment... housing... street gutter... second warning letter... never had this discussion...'

Once Salvignol disappeared, silence resumed at 9 Rue du Vau-l'Eau. Sylvain's mind wavered. Only one thought remained: the betrayal of Odon Gadelorge.

The injured Wolf laid on his side, body limp, breath short. His eyes filled with tears. 'My friend.'

CHAPTER 3

When a Magdelonais meets another Magdelonais, the speaks only of the cold. Not only it had started in the fall, but it also continued. The temperatures on the month of February were at record heights, or rather at the abyss below zero. Some nights, they drop down to -18°. This was the carnage among the weak and old town. The funeral party rubbed their hands.

Sylvain heard the bells ringing. They called her. But it was over, he no longer begged. He imagined Marie-Jeanne Languerrand as a wandering patroness, 'My God, where is my poor man?'

He did not need to beg. He got 30 Euros per session in posing for Odon Gadelorge. He was paid straight. At first it was daily; now, it was for every two or three days.

On the night that followed the discovery of the body, Sylvain had a revelation: 'Gadelorge didn't betray me! That bitch bluffed!' Indeed, by reconstructing the sequence of events, it was not clear at what point Salvignol would have had time to meet Gadelorge. The police were present all that time. Alternatively Odon Gadelorge was a victim, too, of Salvignol's blackmail. 'No, no, no, Odon Gadelorge didn't betray me.' He was convinced. Denial, hypothesis or reality, essentially Sylvain was to continue to drink with his friend in his studio, this great bazaar which was too good to let go of.

When Nadar was buried a month ago, Sylvain hastily concluded that the doctor had proved the obvious: Josée Nadar had died of her phlebitis, nothing suspicious. Odon and Sylvain never spoke of it to each other, not the slightest allusion. As for the press, usually fond of various gruesome facts, it pouted. Nadar had been squashed, in a nutshell.

The most surprising story was that the police have still not summoned him. He wondered if this would explain it: he has had no news of Edgar Huggins, while the latter had to contact him at the end of the Nadar case. Should that case not be over? He retained some guidelines of the rules established by Huggins. The most imperative: stop following him, do not try to contact him, wait for him to call, and above all keep quiet. Duly noted.

He vacuumed, maddening gymnastics with the extension cord several meters long – the only outlet was on the ground floor – that made it knot and gets stuck somewhere.

He was at the second floor landing when the annoying smell heralded the likely arrival of Bérengère Salvignol. It was definitely her; and she puttered, as usual. This was the first time she spoke to him since their brief discussion, if one could call it a discussion.

'Good morning, Mr. Wolf. I have someone interested in viewing the second floor apartment. Should you meet, have the decency not to say that an old lady died here. Common sense. Are we in agreement?'

It was not a question, but a statement. Besides, she did not expect an answer and continued:

'This person will be coming soon. Store your vacuum cleaner.'

Sylvain resisted the urge to reply, 'At your service!' In silence, he began to wrap its extension cord.

He liked his cubbyhole, a closed space of three meters long, under the stairs. That was his secret annex. Salvignol gave him a new lock on the day he was hired. She forgot to keep the duplicate key – all the better. He was happy to be the only one to have access to this cache where the crammed jumble of equipment he needed for maintaining the building: cleaning products, a stool, a box of light bulbs, work clothes, and above all, a multitude of tools and handyman things. Perhaps they were from his predecessor.

He was then fussing over in tidying his vacuum, when he heard a noise clicking above his head -- someone was walking up the stairs. It occurred to him too late to see the individual, but early enough to see part: he has seen this firecracker. It was of Guylaine Monteil, the librarian. He was sure of it!

She would be the future tenant of Nadar's apartment?

Chance? Sylvain was thoughtful.

While he cleaned the pavement of the corridor in the vault decorated by icicles, the two women come down, and he caught bits of dialog: overview, key handover. The business seemed to have concluded. They pass in front of him – as if he were barely there – and they go their separate ways in an exchange of courtesies and bows.

'I have you, you belong to me, I slowly penetrate you, I feel that it's coming, don't move.'

When he paints, Odon Gadelorge used erotic language of which he was unaware; unless this was his fantasy. Whatever, Sylvain did not mind. Nothing bothered him so as he can share good times with Gadelorge.

Neither knows who the other. They never asked questions. Not the past nor the present. To be together, that was enough for them. They held each other in esteem. This was the story of two taciturn individuals who respected each other; empathy in a relationship.

Sylvain's first portrait was relegated to a corner of the workshop, a work in progress. There were two others, sketched from other angles and other light sources; to be set aside. Now was no longer a general view. Sylvain posed sitting on a stool, wearing a white grandpa shirt, casually unbuttoned by half, exposing the junction of a shoulder and part of his torso. The shirt was half-tucked in black trousers. The clothes were too big for Sylvain who remained thin, even when he had enough to eat every day. Odon Gadelorge unearthed them from a garage sale. He was excited the day of its discovery. 'Finally! Here is the subject of my next painting! There he is! There he is!'

Sylvain no longer had his shaved head as in the early days of his arrival. Some six months were enough for a mop of gray hair to, to the delight of Odon Gadelorge, who fluffs it before each session. 'Romantic, my dear, I want you romantic,' he said while cursing having trouble recreating the same hairstyle as the day before or the day before that. The pose consisted of having his left elbow rest on a table, his chin resting on fist. The scene, set near the window, was illuminated only by the light of day. He had to have a dreamy gaze, eyes turned skyward. Dreaming for two hours without doing anything, Sylvain can do.

Ambient silence was broken by a huge ruckus in the stairwell.

'No doubt the new tenant moving on the second floor.'

'No doubt.' the artist replied absently.

The session lasted for a quarter of an hour more.

The bottle of absinthe came; two small rounds and then they part ways; every man for himself; Odon studio bound, Sylvain staircase bound.

On the floor below, the apartment door of the late Josée Nadar was wide open. He lingered on the landing to take a sly look. Walls, stripped of their wallpapers overloaded with old rose peonies on old brown background, were painted white. The oak beams, once in khaki green, have been sanded and coated with a matt varnish. The green curled linoleum disappeared, revealing oak floors. Fresh paint, beeswax and turpentine neutralized the foul odors permanently.

Two movers had difficulty negotiating a bend in the stairwell with a bed base 160 cm wide. They fulminated, stuck between the first and second floor and found the trick and continue their ascent. Sylvain had always admired those skilled in the art. They did not even need to be buff, it was know-how and gumption that held their strength.

Out came Guylaine Monteil, dashing in her red tracksuit dating from a bygone era when she was two sizes smaller.

'Good Morning! Oooooh, gosh, I know you! But yes, you are Mr. Wolf!'

The feint was coarse, and the actress played badly, Sylvain responded with a lack of energy.

'Yes, hello.'

'And you live here?'

'I am the caretaker of the building.'

'How funny! You are of course aware that I moved in today in this apartment.'

While flirting, she pointed to the open door with a wave of her arm, which was also an invitation for him to come in. Sylvain pretended not to understand and quickly went go down the stairs, leaving no time for Guylaine Monteil to continue her cooing.

The door of the lodge opened with the noise of crumpled paper. A newspaper page folded in four was trapped under the threshold bar. First, it was hard to remove it without tearing. He could turn from one side and the other, yet he did not see why anyone bothered to drop him this piece of junk, dated that same day. Finally, he discovered on the margin, elegantly written words in Huggins' hand and fountain pen: 'Tonight 21:00. Same place. Come with this newspaper page.'

In his own place, Sylvain had a habit of thinking aloud, 'What a drama queen! Can't do like everyone else, that guy.'

The cold was less intense in the recent days. But it was devious. Temperatures, near freezing during day, favored snowfall. Negative by night, they leave all that time for the snow to freeze, forming drifts. Good to *Au Bon Bouilleur* at 21:00 through the suburbs of the Ville-Basse swept by a whipping wind – it was not the most tempting prospect.

In time, Sylvain first prepared his stomach with a bowl of soup brick and a bread-butter-camembert, washed down with a quarter of red. At this hour, most of the blinds and shutters were closed. The Magdelonais protect themselves from the cold and from looks. However, for some windows with transparent curtains, there were atmospheres. Couples or families were unaware, but they all looked together in the same direction, their eyes fixed on the TV that sucked out their brains.

Without having crossed anyone in the streets, Sylvain arrived near the *Bon Bouilleur* a quarter of an hour in advance and remained on the other side of the avenue, where he began to briskly pace back and forth.

At 21:00, a dark and muddy gray Volvo station wagon pulled up in front of the bistro. Edgar Huggins came out. The break restarted too fast, the front tires skidded on ice, beginning a spin. The driver rectified the controlled vehicle and moved away slowly in an icebreaker noise.

When Huggins began to rummage in the door locks, Sylvain joined him. It was not even a good night. The man in the hat had swapped his raincoat with a beige coat with a black velvet collar.

After turning on the gaslamp, Huggins asked him to wait a moment, and it felt like an order. With a candle, he passed through a door covered with a multi-colored plastic curtain behind the bar.

The ghosts of the *Bon Bouilleur* were still there, leaning on the counter, the privileged place for small talk and gossip. Sylvain saw and heard: 'And a little black, and a white, a half pressure, and one cognac, one!' They peeled smelly boiled eggs and nibbled too salty peanuts in sticky saucers teeming with big old microbes, all fiddling with both hands after pissed. Some were seated, playing dominoes or cards, rounds making rounds. 'Hey boss, you give that back!' They would be appalled if they were told to drink in moderation. 'In moderation? Where's that?' Dismayed that they were forbidden to smoke. 'You know where I'll put that smoking ban?' Dismayed that their bistro would be harmed, 'You hear that, boss? We can drink more, we can more smoke. You can close your shop! Come on, let's light this up and make it flow!'

They were still trying to laugh when Edgar Huggins broke the mood with his party-pooper face. He had a package under his arm and a bottle of whiskey, which he poured in two big glasses.

'First of all, Mr Wolf, have you thought to bring my newspaper?'

'Sylvain handed him the paper. When he saw Huggins take it, disappearing behind the counter and burning it in the sink, he was not even surprised. In this very unearthly environment, nothing was extravagant.

Edgar Huggins started to pontificate:

'Now, Mr Wolf, I advise you to listen to me carefully. Learn not to say anything when a policeman asks you questions. I had to intervene to prevent the opening of an investigation into the death of Josée Nadar. I also had to calm the press down. I close my eyes for this one. Recognize that this was a blunder on your part. But you have no room for error. Isn't that right, Mr. Wolf?'

Sylvain did not consider it necessary to reply. Huggins was still annoying with his 'Isn't that right, Mr. Wolf?' – a verbal tic, or a fine strategy to unsettle him.

Huggins put on the table a padded envelope the size of a two-hundred-page paperback, closed with several rounds of packaging tape.

'I entrust this package to you. You will wear it tonight at the address I'll tell you. Understand?'

'Up to that point, yes.'

'The man who will welcome you will ask, "What was the weather like in the Atlantic?" You will answer, " A little choppy with a moderate swell." He will not say anything more, and neither will you. You must not get inside his house, all you'll do is deliver. You still with me?'

'Yes'

'You will go home right away. Nothing else to do this time. That will not even take you an hour. If all goes as planned, you will receive 100 Euros. Compared to your hourly minimum wage that's good enough, right?'

Sylvain strived to remain expressionless. His dull eyes watched the other without seeing him in turn. To compose himself, he took a sip. He said nothing.

'Do you know where Rue des Rouets is?' Huggins resumed.

'Yes.'

'A single-storey house at No. 27. You're expected. Hurry up.'

A last swig of whiskey and Sylvain was already up.

'One moment, please.' Huggins stopped him. 'Of course, nothing happened tonight. But it's needless to remind you, I'm sure. Isn't that right, Mr. Wolf? Wait until I call for you again.'

Sylvain held the envelope in the waistband of his pants, as if it were a gun. Who would've thought? Without a word, without a glance, he was masterful when it came to stepping out of the place of darkness, leaving behind the snotty man. Finally out, he sing-songed: 'Dear Mr. Huggins, I too, can do drama.' He resumed his humble stance when when he carefully placed his crepe soles on the slippery ground.

Forced walk slowly, it took half an hour to reach Rue des Rouets. At No. 27, the front of the house had a door arched by a canopy and two shuttered windows. It appeared to be an abandoned building, with its run down plaster, beat-up gutter hanging and screeching every breath of wind.

He took the ring-shaped door knocker. He waited. He knocked again. Someone finally opened. With their imposing stature, they could be a man. The individual wore a fur hat, and her face was crushed under a stocking. Good. Sylvain could do masquerades, too.

Disciplined, he readied himself to play coded sentences.

'What was the weather like in the Atlantic?' whispered the other.

'A little choppy, with a moderate swell.' Sylvain matched the confidential tone.

They took the envelope from him, and slammed the door in his face.

Now he had one thing in mind, and only one: to be in bed Sleep was another thing entirely.

Among the things he found in his cubbyhole, Sylvain found a small plywood panel with a hole through which was threaded a string, and held a handwritten note: 'The caretaker will be back in an hour or two.' It was better than the traditional' the concierge back soon.' – provided, of course, not to specify the start time. He took care to hang the panel on the handle of his front door to go to his appointment.

Back to Rue du Vau-L'Eau at around 21:00, he was surprised: Maryse Beurdelet was there before his office. It must be serious if she showed up at night, wearing a pale pink kimono robe. She floated in, and her face was rather pallid.

'I was expecting you, Mr. Wolf. I heard footsteps in the attic above my house. Could you come and see...'

Alarm gave more human side to Beurdelet.

'I'm coming, Miss.'

Sylvain dove into his cubbyhole and got tangled in a jumble of disparate objects, triggering noisy landslides. After a close fight, he came out triumphant with a stool. He also carried a flashlight and a rat trap. The sight thrilled Maryse Beurdelet.

She spoke softly as she headed up the stairs in front of Sylvain, her foot catching in her robe:

'They were heavy footsteps... I could've sworn someone was walking up there.'

A hatch above the fourth floor landing gave access to the attic. Sylvain climbed the ladder, pushing the door with a snap, and before venturing there, swept the light of the flashlight in the space. That was the first time he visited the attic. The frame was made of reddish brown chestnut. Dust balls and the cobwebs hung from the beams forming dusty curtains. The l'œil de bœuf with broken windows let moonlight in, illuminating a thick layer of pigeon droppings. The presence of small rodents was confirmed by wool nests, as well as many black droppings. Debris of carcasses and bones hint at a small passing predator, also identified by its characteristic droppings: twisted with a tapered tip, and a distinctive length. It was a weasel.

When Sylvain was about to go down, he stopped short, intrigued by a light at ground level. He pushed away the skullduggery obstructing his source of light and lay on his stomach to examine it more closely. It was a narrow gap along Maryse Beurdelet's bathroom ceiling: a direct view of the sink and the bathtub. 'Wow!' He enthused in advance, before rejoining Beurdelet who worried at the foot of the ladder.

'Well?'

'It was just a weasel who hunts mice. I just have replace the broken windows. The animal could've gone through that. I'll lay down traps. Meanwhile, you can rest easy.'

'Are you sure?'

'Sure.'

Maryse Beurdelet was thoughtful. She opened her mouth to say something, changed her mind, and bundled up in her giant bathrobe. She had already replaced her usual rigid mask when she closed her armored door.

'Thank you, Mr. Wolf. That would be all.'

Sylvain's night was a series of daydreams interspersed with short periods of deep sleep. At dawn, he feelt motivated to take care of the attic, but preferred to wait for Maryse Beurdelet to leave before heading up there. He will take care of the windows – they were in quarter circles, not easy to install. In addition, the skylight without hinges was fixed, which will force him to work on site (ah yes) and be back several times (ah yes).

Shortly after Beurdelet's departure at 08:30 on the dot, he was in the attic flat on a wool moth-bitten blanket: a discovery in his cubbyhole. There actually was a structure between the attic floor and ceiling latch on the fourth floor. The crack was sufficient to keep a discreet eye out, provided that he took care that dust did not fall into the tub. That would give away the presence of the hole and that of the watchman at the same time. With a finger, he cautiously cleaned the periphery of the slot.

Sylvain needed the agreement of the owner for the purchase of four custom glass windows, mouse traps for rats, dormice, and other rodents. It was time for his posing session with Odon Gadelorge, and he took the opportunity to find Salvignol.

The artist had a cold and was cranky. He announced at the outset, in a concert of sniffling and nose-blowing, that the day's session will not last more than an hour. Sylvain gave up on asking if he can use the phone. This was not the time. He quickly put on his work clothes, buttoned the shift by mistake, then unbuttoned it right away to expose his chest, and then applied himself to take the same position as the previous sessions. To help him, Gadelorge painted in gouache the location of his elbow on the table. The artist arranged the vast neckline of the shirt in his way, in which the flaps must be there and not there, then got upset about Sylvain's hair. All that remained to do was to show the dying romantic air seasoned by Gadelorge, before settling comfortably in his fantasies, his thoughts set on the attic.

Not even three minutes later, Odon Gadelorge's anger set Sylvain's thoughts tumbling two floors below.

'Confound it, Mr Wolf, stop with that stupid smile! I cannot work under these conditions!'

'Oh! Sorry.'

Gadelorge lowered his tone seeing Sylvain's sheepish face.

'Let's cancel this session. This is not my day. Yours neither, apparently. Come back tomorrow at the same time.'

A burst of sneezing and a shot of absinthe followed.

18:30: he awaited the arrival of Maryse Beurdelet.

18:30: she arrived.

He went into stringy explanations. He has not yet talked to the owner, he had no telephone, he could not take care of the attic as...

'I told Miss Salvignol. You make a quote and you send it to me.' she interrupted him.

And she concluded with an administrative letter template.

'I expect that you will do the necessary work as soon as possible.'

He liked it better when Beurdelet was scared.

Sylvain no longer went to the market since Nadar's death. He did not go to church to beg since the meeting with Marie Jeanne Languerrand, no longer milled around since Edgar Huggins noticed him. His trips were limited to the discount store located ten minutes away from Rue du Vau-L'Eau, where he did all his groceries.

In the afternoon, he was content to walk, although there were some signs of snow, thus the gray twilight. The DIY store of Puits-Magdelon was located at Place de la Gare, after a straight avenue between two rows of bicentennial plane trees. On each side, old houses of notable people stood, most of them have two floors and double staircases. They were pulled back, away from the sidewalk by closed gardens of fences and wrought iron gates. Some were renovated that disfigures the original house. Others were just holding on with their cracks, leaks and damaged roofs. Gray stone facades line up as symbols of prestige of their owners, so proud to flaunt the they call 'success in life'. As for houses too old to be inhabited, they were not lost for everybody: they have their squatters.

The Puits-Magdelon passenger station has been abandoned for many years. On the railways, long strings of freight cars that pass by were reminiscent of armyworms. Grain convoys were frequent and regular, allowing nostalgic Magdelonais hear the train whistle.

When Sylvain went to the hardware store, he noticed a car parked nearby. It rang him a bell. The image of the car was superimposed over what he had seen on the night of his second appointment with Huggins: the same dark gray Volvo station wagon, even if muddy. It would therefore be tracked and monitored. Whatever floats their boat, he said to himself, pretending to have seen nothing.

At that point nothing bothered him, and he entered a world that was right for him: that of amateur tinkerers. In the aisles of the vast store, customers in the inner circle were at home and know what they want. They were recognized by their professional gestures. Beginners, smaller, their questions posed to teachers or condescending sellers. Sylvain loiter among the shelves, stopped to daydream of gardening tools. One day he will get back to gardening again, his gardener business. He promised to himself.

'Mr. Wolf! You, here!'

He knew that voice, he knew that face, but where has he ever seen that face? A painstaking scan of the recesses of his memory gradually pulled up the image of the butcher in the market, so difficult to recognize outside the performance of his duties and his white apron.

'I heard of Madame Nadar's death. She was very sick, it seemed. Another of our old who has left. And since then you haven't come to market?'

'No,' said Sylvain without seeing the need to say more.

Intuitively, it was suspicious. It made him wonder if this guy disguised himself as a good man, if he wasn't being monitored, him too.

The butcher resumes.

'That's too Bad. My colleagues and I will wait for you whenever you feel like coming back. Until we see each other again, Mr. Wolf!'

'Goodbye, Mr., uh ...'

'Jeannot Marchadier, at your service.'

Sylvain went to meet a seller in a red jacket. Quote for the manufacture of glass and traps. There, it was done.

'To whom should I name the quote?'

'Sylvain Wolf.'

'W-o-l-f. Like a wolf?'

At the station square, the dark gray station wagon was gone. It was snowing.

The time was up when Maryse Beurdelet was bewildered and humanized in her pink terry bathrobe, and she spoke to him. Every time he came across her, she took on an offended air and walked like an ostrich. He deposited the DIY store's quotation in her mailbox, and waits for the next steps. No news for three days.

At the end of the day, after a posing session at Gadelorge's he found a paper on the floor of his lodge. A letter from Bérengère Salvignol perhaps? No. This was another kind of message: 'Tonight 21:00. Same place. Come with this newspaper page.' No varied in his methods, Mr. Huggins.

Sylvain had dinner before his appointment: sauerkraut, beer. In forty-eight hours, the outside temperature has climbed about ten degrees. Piles of dirty snow accumulated in the streets, melting fast. Sylvain patted about in the thick slush and avoided the sides of houses because of the water streams falling uninterrupted from their roofs.

He arrived at *Bon Bouilleur* several minutes early.

At 21:00, nothing moved inside the pub.

He dared to knock at the door. Edgar Huggins opened immediately, as if he was stuck behind it. He admitted Sylvain in, but did not invite him to sit. The room was plunged into darkness. The ghosts were silent.

With impatience in his voice, jerky movements, Huggins has everything worth a hurried or worried man.

'Give me your newspaper page, first.'

Sylvain moved with voluntarily displayed calm. Huggins handed him the same envelope similar to that of the last time.

'To be delivered straight to 11 Avenue de la Gare. To the question "What was the weather like in the Atlantic?" You reply, "Storm warning." Hurry. At our next appointment, you will be paid for both deliveries. Both or nothing.'

Sylvain felt pushed out by a firm hand on his back, a gesture he disliked. It was a discreet shove. He said nothing and left.

At 11 Avenue de La Gare, stood a seemingly abandoned house: a dead tree in a snowy garden bristled in brambles, roof partially collapsed, rotten shutters, windows broken. Probably a squatter. The gate was open, the door was ajar, and someone was lurking. Sylvain settled at the foot of the steps.

'Who were you?' asked a female voice.

Ah! The question was not provided in the program. Should he respond?

'Uh ... a delivery.'

'Go away!' She expected no delivery.

He hesitated, then dared to ask.

'Don't you want to know the weather in the Atlantic?

'I told you to leave.' shouted the voice.

He heard a window that opened from the house next door. Sylvain gave up.

Back in his lodgings, he wrote with a red ballpoint pen in the margin of a sheet of newspaper: 'Delivery impossible.' Then he bent over backwards and slipped it into Edgar Huggins' mailbox. He still did not understand the value of using cut newspapers for messages – another Hugginsian folklore. Finally, he enclosed the envelope in a zippered pocket of his backpack and tossed it at the bottom of the cabinet.

Five o'clock in the morning. He got up up, turned on the gas to heat leftover coffee in a small saucepan. All of Sylvain's dishes came from garage sales in Puits-Magdelon. He also found a new radio/CD player for 4 Euros, two lamps with their shades for 3 Euros, a carton full of books for 50 cents, a bunch of towels, sheets and wool blankets for 8 Euros bargained for, 6.50 Euros; and then his clothes, his shoes, everything.

There were two letters for him under the door, probably delivered by funny night owls. He heard nothing. First, the newspaper page in return. Where Sylvain wrote 'delivery impossible' Edgar Huggins crossed out the word 'impossible' and added: 'At 11 am this morning, same address. Return this newspaper page in my mailbox.' Second-mail: a closed envelope. Inside were a blank check to the hardware store, and a few sentences on a post-it: 'Okay for the quote. Fill the exact amount and make an invoice in my name. Take care of everything immediately. B. Salvignol.'

The coffee was currently at rolling boil, giving off a smell of grilled chicken droppings.

Logically, he would deliver the Avenue de la Gare envelope before going to the hardware store. As he was three minutes ahead, he was in front of the house, which seemed to him less imposing in the day than at night. The snow has melted, revealing rows of disheveled boxwood, lanky roses, dead shrubs and a network of brambles entangled in tall discolored grass. He could see himself tearing, cutting, weeding, hoeing, replanting. The garden gate was opened. Sylvain went to the porch, when he heard a voice behind him:

'Looking for something?

From the avenue, a morose teenager came toward him, head buried in two superimposed hoods.

'I don't know.' responded Sylvain, simply.

'So, fuck off!'

'The weather in the Atlantic, doesn't it interest you?'

'Aren't your brains a little scrambled? Get out, I said. If you don't, I'll get my buddies.'

The teen with the empty look in his eyes stared Sylvain out of the garden, and waddled towards the entrance of the house.

Sylvain took the direction of Place de la Gare, but stopped after a few meters. It would be better not to keep him on the trail of Edgar Huggins. U-turn. In the avenue, there was a burning smell. It was No. 11. A thick yellow smoke came out of an upstairs window. The windows were shattered and releasing raging flames. Whoa, there!

Sylvain shouted several times 'Fire!', running in all directions on the sidewalks and in the middle of the roadway. Nothing moved in the neighboring houses. Someone finally carefully opened a window, a little but not too much. 'Call the fire department!' Yelled Sylvain. The individual continued to spy without showing themselves.

Finally, a car stops, opened its window. A man in a suit and tie holding a mobile phone glued to his ear. When Sylvain joined, he was currently specifying the address to the fire rescue center. It was a fifty-year old man with a youthful face, hair looking as if he just came out of the bath, and his Mom has combed it with a side part.

'Has it been blazing long?' he asked calmly.

'Two or three minutes.'

'And you did not warn firefighters?'

'I don't have a mobile phone.'

'Really? That's rare.'

The flames' roar intensified, the blaze was so furious, that it could burn one's face, even if he stood at several meters away. The structural beams were already falling inside the house in a roar whose echo reverberated throughout the avenue. The show was terrifying, but beautiful, or terrifying because it was beautiful. It was no longer clear for Sylvain.

Very soon, coming from nowhere, curious onlookers gathered. They're like flies, thought Sylvain. We don't see just one, and they come out of nothing as soon as there was shit somewhere.

Return to Rue du Vau-L'Eat. Return of the envelope in the pocket of the backpack at the bottom of the cabinet. To mess with Huggins, he did not writing on a newspaper page, but rather on a notebook page: 'Second delivery impossible.' Into the mister's mailbox. To be continued.

Street side, the door of the building opened, Guylaine Monteil, short-dressed, made a waggling entry. She really was the opposite of Beurdelet.

'Good morning, Mr. Wolf. I have a favor to ask of you.'

He would say no. However, the last time he tried to refuse service to a tenant, it was with Nadar, and he saw what he saw, and how far it has led. He responds with suspicion and restraint.

'If it's up my alley.'

'I have pictures to hang on the wall, but I have no drill. Do you have one?'

'Yes.'

'I dare not use it myself. Could you help me?

'Okay,' Sylvain answered softly. 'I'll be there.'

'Why not tonight, at 18:00?'

'Perhaps, if I have time.'

Sylvain will not be at Guylaine Monteil's at 18:00. He will be at the gendarmerie of Puits-Magdelon, in hot water. Very hot water.

CHAPTER 4

With all his adventures, he was not able to go shopping that morning, that it delayed his taking care of the attic. It was a Saturday. He would return to the store in the afternoon. Then he will begin to install the windows of the œil de bœuf. It will not be finished once the sun sets, so he will come back the next morning – with the hope to be there at the right time to catch Maryse Beurdelet's Sunday pampering. Sylvain hung his panel to the door handle: 'The concierge is gone for an hour or two.'

To go to the hardware store, he had to go through Avenue de La Gare. It was the only way. At the place of the fire, there was a security perimeter and a lot of commotion. Firefighters searched the still smoldering rubble. Two policemen were there. A small group of journalists willing to settle for any crumb of information, and sew them to the seam of their pants. Also present were the inevitable onlookers. The roof collapsed between the blackened walls – still standing but decapitated. The openings without their joints evoke the eyes of the dead, when they need to be closed.

Sylvain recognized the teenager he met that morning. From a distance, he saw him shrug, squirming in his oversized sneakers, making faces while answering to inquisitive gendarmes. Sylvain has already seen those two: they came to Rue du Vau-L'Eau the day of the discovery of the body Nadar's body.

Suddenly, the teen looked lively, his face lit up as he showed Sylvain with a finger insistently. The stockier of the two gendarmes come striding towards a motionless Sylvain. A journalist was little a few steps away, their microphone held out.

'Hello, sir,' opens the gendarme. 'I have some questions to ask you. It seems that you were present this morning at 11 am, at the time of the fire?'

'Yes, I went to the hardware store at the Place de la Gare.'

'Do you know the young man over there?'

'No.'

'Have you ever been in this house?'

'No.'

'Did you see the fire?'

'Yes, I saw it start. I shouted "Fire"!' as much as I could. No one moved in the neighborhood. It took several minutes until someone passed by in a car and called the fire department with his mobile phone.'

'Someone?'

'Yes, a man.'

'You will follow us, sir. We'll clear this up.'

He walked beside the gendarme who held him firmly by the arm. A nervous woman referred to Sylvain in grand gestures while talking with another policeman. The journalist with the microphone approached the woman slyly. Sylvain and the teenager were shoved into the paddy wagon. Photos. Cameras. The stocky policeman stayed with them. The other policeman, the great sportsman at top of the class, took the wheel. On the other side of the avenue were delighted onlookers. There was a lot going on in Puits-Magdelon.

He was alone in a windowless room for some time: maybe two hours, maybe more. It was not a cell, but rather a place reserved for interrogation, with a table and two chairs. With no television, Sylvain never looked at police series. At that moment, he felt that it lacked culture. He did not know his rights, did not really know what was happening or how far it can go. After a long identity verification, his pockets emptied and jacket removed, he was then locked in the room without a word to him. That was all. He waited. The bare bulb in the ceiling reached an uncanny number of watts e. He preferred to keep his eyes closed. He sat at the table, his chest rocked and his head fell on his arms. He fell asleep. He felt stifled in a blast of heat. The walls of the room with no windows began to undulate strangely. There were sparks. They arose spontaneously from the ground, climbed the walls, licked, hopped, sparkled, rose, rose, rose like a little beast ...

A burst interrupted Sylvain's dream. A friendly looking man sat in front of him. His face was pleasant while being greatly asymmetrical: one eye lower than the other, a crooked nose and a mouth with a tugged corner; a model that would please Odon Gadelorge for his next picture.

'I am Commissioner Gauthier, chief of the district police. I had to drive to come up Puits-Magdelon, that was why you waited. Okay, let's get to the point. The fire in the Avenue de la Gare killed two people. Just that. Firefighters have already determined that it was arson. You were seen at the scene three times. First: the night before the fire. It was past 21:00, you were in the garden, at the foot of the steps. You were talking to someone on the inside of the house, who was said to have screamed in fear and asking you to leave. At that time, you were illuminated by a street lamp, and a neighbor saw you. She acknowledged that without hesitation this afternoon. Secondly, this morning, at around 11:00, you have again gone into the garden of the house. A young man had also asked you to leave and have had to insist. You were "seriously weird," he told me. He also formally recognized you. Third, the same neighbor saw you yelling fire at the precise moment when a man arrived by car and phoned the fire brigade. That's a lot stuff, sir. What were you doing in this house?'

Sylvain was torn. He had not forgotten Edgar Huggins' threats. Shut up, he can only be silent! However, the more he was silent, the longer it took the risk of being convicted of a fire that killed two people. He wanted to tell this Gauthier everything: the strange Mr. Huggins, the honorary mayor, the industrial zone, the haunted bistro *Au Bon Bouilleur*, the muddy station wagon, the feeling of being followed, deliveries, Euros, the man with a stocking over his head, abandoned houses, burned newspaper pages, threats of torture and death... everything, everything, everything. Even the murder of Josée Nadar? No, everything but the murder;

that's for later, if – and only if – he can no longer do otherwise.

To explain the blackmail he suffered, he simply had to tell the Commissioner Gauthier another scenario, also true: Edgar Huggins blackmailed him because he was seen begging; the owner will turn on him if she learns of it; he will not lose his job and his lodgings; he was ready to do anything not to go back to the street; Edgar Huggins has understood this and played on it.

Commissioner Gauthier awaited the response to his question, without showing his impatience, with his eyes downcast and a pensive pout on his lips, his hands folded were on the table. He was the portrait of a serene man. 'He's probably ten years younger than me, but his maturity must be ten times as much.' Sylvain told himself.

'You want some coffee?' asked Gauthier.

'Yes.'

This diversion was to Sylvain's advantage.

'Two coffees, if you please,' ordered Gauthier casually on the phone. A young policeman, happy to show his zeal, showed up – hey presto! – with two steaming cups.

'Listen to me, Mr. Wolf. This fire, I think you had nothing to do with it, but I'm alone in thinking that. Everyone's accusing you. I don't even see how you could prove your innocence. The gendarmes prancing behind the door are waiting for the green light to place you in custody. They'll have a bonus, compliments of the chief, for their quick response. They haven't interrogated you yet because I told them to do nothing before my arrival. If I steal their prey, I won't be responsible for your fate. So you had better agree with me. Know that the two individuals who died in the fire were small cannabis dealers. The police know them. They had never more than three grams on them when they were arrested and were therefore released. This is a much more dangerous guy, a trader at the head of an organized network, who has been eliminated. Burned alive. They were gagged and tied together with wire, in a locked room. You can just imagine their ways. You were there at the wrong time. But that did not tell me what you came do. Were you buying drugs or bringing them?

'Bringing them. Maybe.'

'Maybe?'

'I don't have the right to know what was in the packages I deliver. This one was the second. I couldn't give it to the recipient.'

'Can you tell me?'

Oh yes, Sylvain could tell him that!

At the beginning, words failed him, he became a bumbling bundle of language. Then everything was unlocked and it was a verbal diarrhea. To be listened to by someone, he did not know what that was, so he grabbed the opportunity, even if it was hard to hide his doubts. He told his story. It was also a way to answering. He was himself, and that was it. He left no detail overlooked.

Commissioner Gauthier, diving throughout the story, let out a long whistle.

'You're in a worse mess than I imagined. Are you willing to work in exchange for police protection?'

'I don't know.'

'You don't know? You really don't know? Listen, Mr. Wolf, you make me think of a virgin who entered a

BDSM club without her knowing it. You have set foot in an environment of which you know nothing about. Now you're forced to stay because you won't come out alive: you know too much. If this Edgar Huggins was the individual we were looking for in the past few years – and it's a very strong likelihood – I can tell you how he gets rid of those he no longer needs. Are you up for it?

'No.'

'Here's the deal: you become my informant. In return, I close the fire case, so you're cleared of all suspicion. Then you avoid jail for your dealer activity. For that was what you did, right? Even if you want to pretend that you don't understand it, even if it was under pressure from a blackmailer. For the prosecutor and the judge, you're a drug dealer – a big one, given the amount you're carrying. With my proposal, you have everything to gain. Sure, we're taking big risks now, but not only will you take no more, but you'll have the protection of the authorities. So you'll continue your 'mission', keeping me informed of everything, such as: your appointment with Huggins, shipping addresses, etc. I will give you a cell phone exclusively for communications with me.'

'And if Huggins thinks I've talked to someone?' Sylvain asked.

'In that case, you're dead soon as you take one step out of the gendarmerie.'

'So?'

'So, you go home. Edgar Huggins will do you nothing until he has not recovered his precious envelope. Does that work with you?'

'That works.' responded Sylvain, unconvinced.

The operation of the mobile phone and charger was explained to him. He listened carefully: this was his first cell phone. Commissioner Gauthier had just pulled it out of his pocket as quickly as a magician pulled a rabbit out of a hat. To call him, Sylvain simply had to dial 01.

Last instructions, last precautions.

'For my part, I won't be calling you. If you ever receive a call, don't pick it up and let me know immediately. And above all, don't use the phone to call someone other than myself.'

Crossing the gendarmerie, Sylvain saw the teenager handcuffed and visibly proud of it. He made himself passive, and he was dragged down the hallway by an annoyed policewoman. Sylvain met the gaze of the two gendarmes who booked him. He found them a little grumpy.

On the way back, he thought to buy the TV in the next garage sale.

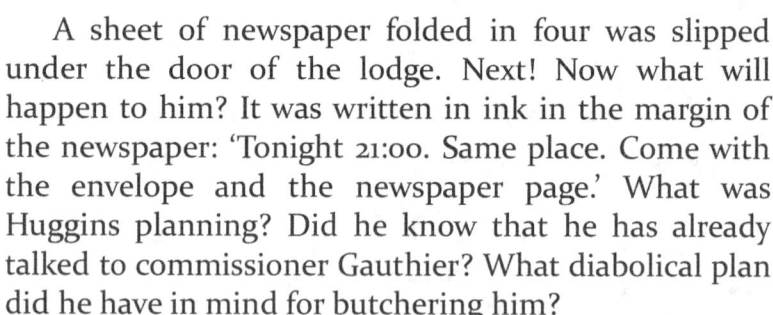

A sheet of newspaper folded in four was slipped under the door of the lodge. Next! Now what will happen to him? It was written in ink in the margin of the newspaper: 'Tonight 21:00. Same place. Come with the envelope and the newspaper page.' What was Huggins planning? Did he know that he has already talked to commissioner Gauthier? What diabolical plan did he have in mind for butchering him?

In less than a second, he dialed 01 on the mobile phone. The Commissioner picked up at the end of the same second. Sylvain read out Huggins' message.

'This is not the time to back out, alright?' said Gauthier as he heard Sylvain's hesitant voice.

'No, yes, I'll go.'

'You're not alone, remember that.'

It was time to deliver the ordered meals. He knews what he wanted, and he has long dreamed about it: a pizza. Near Rue du Vau-L'Eau, a pizzeria sold pizzas for take away.

'A Royale, please.'

'The large or small?'

'The laaaarge one.'

Tonight was party -- especially if it was to be the last.

If Huggins set their appointment at *Bon Bouilleur*, it was a good sign because he would not have taken the risk to meet him at that address if he was suspected of having ratted him out to the Commissioner Gauthier, Sylvain reassured himself the best he could. He walked quickly, avoiding the puddles, still stagnant here and there after the snow had melted.

At 21:00, he knocked on the door of the *Bon Bouilleur*. Edgar Huggins opened right away. Sylvain snuck in, hiding his shaking hands in his pockets. In passing, he gave Huggins a quick glance: he thought he saw a smile. It was so unexpected that his anxiety soared. The gas lamp was on, the bottle of whiskey and two glasses were placed on a table.

'Do you have the envelope and the newspaper?' he asked, extending his hand. 'Do you know why I use newspapers for my mail? It was no longer anonymous: a paper for the general public, which was discarded after use. Just like toilet paper. Ha! Ha! Hahaha!'

Sylvain did not like that laugh. He handed the envelope over along with the newspaper, with a gesture sharper than expected. He was quick to put his hands back in his pockets.

'Nice work, Mr. Wolf. You've managed, somehow, to divert the attention of police on a kid. That'll keep them busy. They have their alleged offender for the burning of the Avenue de la Gare. Your delivery attempt went unnoticed. Well played. Alas, for that kid, that's another story. He saw you. I'll take care of him soon enough. I understand that a neighbor had seen you too – too bad for her. The man in the car, who called the firefighters, arrived later because someone called fire. So we can forget it for now.'

How did he know all this? Sylvain wanted to ask whether Huggins had a direct connection with the gendarmerie of Puits-Magdelon – a permanently connected red phone. However, clarification followed that offered temporary comfort to Sylvain.

'I heard the story over the radio. I even saw you on television, regional news. You're already a star. This isn't a problem for the continuation of our business, since you were cleared of all suspicion. The media have something to do: you were a witness in shock, who shouted 'Fire!' to general indifference. That gave them a good scoop,' sneers Huggins.

And journalists have already peddled little they knew, each struggling to be first. Obviously, two dead in the arson of a squatter, it was good for the audience.

Nothing soothed Sylvain's anxiety. There was something new in Edgar Huggins' demeanor, and he did not understand what it was. The blah blah, his way of saying, 'good work' and, 'well played' were not consistent.

Without stopping to pause, Huggins continued.

'You are expected at No. 27 Rue des Rouets, the same address as your first delivery. Someone will ask, "How's the cat?" and you will answer: "Almost healed." This mission will bring 100 Euros, as the previous one. But one does not go without the other. As long as the second delivery is suspended, you will get nothing. Up to you to ensure that things go as they should. That's all for today.'

Under the shadow of his hat, Edgar Huggins threw Sylvain a look of half disdain, half irony. Little detail did not slip Sylvain despite his nervousness: Huggins' deathly look stands out against the colored page of a calendar hanging on the wall behind him. It showed – a drawing or photo? – of a seductive blonde, plump curves hugged by her slinky bright red mini-dress. He recalled a time when roadsters dared to show their favorite women on their windshield, indifferent to feminist ire.

'Again, Mr Wolf, that's all for today. Hurry up.'

Sylvain made a remarkable exit. First he finished his drink, drank too quickly, choking, spitting out everything on the table. He got up – too fast, even – and overturned his chair. It took two tries to pick it up. He hit a table corner as he headed for the door and slammed it close much stronger than he intended to. The bastard must've put something in my whiskey, he said to himself.

Friend, friend, raise your glass, and careful not to spill it! sung the ghosts of *Bon Bouilleur*.

He was alone on the outskirts of Ville-Basse. It was protected by the police – and it was a good secret police. He moved away from several hundred meters looking for a hideout to call and found what he was looking for: a self-flushing pay urinal.

Beep, beep, 01. Direct line to Commissioner Gauthier.

'I'm listening.'

Sylvain told him about his appointment, expressed his foreboding, and also spoke of the threats fired by the teenager and the woman at Avenue de la Gare.

'Go home directly after your delivery. Do not move and call me before leaving tomorrow morning. And stay alone tonight.'

Be alone tonight, it should not be hard.

The houses were as mortal as the generations of mortals they hold. Uninhabited, they did not survive long from their occupants' departure. There were no more living at No. 7 Rue des Rouets, and the cottage was dying.

Sylvain banged the knocker on the door. The fictional character that appears stayed in the shadows. Their nylon stockings over their head, but a ski cap instead of the fur hat. Yes it was less cold than last time.

'How's the cat?'

'Almost healed.'

Clack! The door was closed
The envelope was finally delivered
Not soon enough. Good riddance
Sylvain burped after his pizza

No insomnia that night. Sylvain slept. He got up to heat leftover coffee. He slid two slices of baguette in his brand new 1 Euro toaster. When he was in his kitchen with utensils and dishes gradually bought with his money, he felt socially integrated. In his mind, 'integrated' did mean 'accepted'. Sylvain had no sense of belonging. He had never been part of a group at any level whatsoever: professional, voluntary or friendly. He had always been isolated – a lone Wolf kicked out of the pack.

Wolf has created a forest of green plants inside the lodge. Some were taller than him, others formed an undergrowth. He had them all around the small room. He went around between the pots as if following a forest trail. He felt good with its plants, and the plants are comfortable with him.

It was Sunday. It was no different light at No.9 Rue Vau-L'Eau; except that Maryse Beurdelet was not working. The events of the day have prevented Sylvain from buying windows for the œil de bœuf, but he would still be in the attic that morning. He would clean it thoroughly so that rodents would no longer make it their territory. Besides, what would grab a hungry little rodent in a garage sale?

Sylvain went back to bed until it was time to open the Press House: There certainly had to be an article about the fire in the Sunday edition of the regional newspaper. Then he will wait up to a reasonable time, hours before the mayhem in the attic. When he dozed off, it was always peculiar; he switched between the feeling of falling and the flying. He had two tunes in mind.

His choice.

One went back to his childhood:

La feuille d'automne
Emportée par le vent
En ronde monotone
Tombe en tourbillonnant...

The other was from the Sixties:

Oh m'sieur, oh m'sieur, oh oh m'sieur
Oh dites-moi m'sieur, faites que j'sois un oiseau
Avec des ailes pour m'envoler là-haut...

Up there... there was suddenly a familiar noise: the floor was creaking. Edgar Huggins was home. Sylvain had the habit of looking at the ceiling, as if it allowed him to hear better. Huggins had just got up after spending the night in bed, or has he just returned? He was walking in his apartment, so what? As usual. But for Sylvain, not as usual, he turned in his bed He was afraid. In a flash, he knew why Huggins' attitude seemed different last night. He did not once heard this verbal tic that he used to punctuate one out of three sentences, his famous 'Isn't that right, Mr. Wolf?' The steps stopped. Sylvain remained tense. Silence. He eventually went back to sleep.

When he woke up, he dialed Commissioner Gauthier on the mobile phone.

'Yes?'

'I'm going out to buy the newspaper. After that, I'll clean the attic.'

He spoke as low as possible, hand cupping his mouth, although there was little risk that he could be from upstairs.

'Nothing to report?'

'Nothing.'

'Huggins came home?'

'Yes.'

'Alright. See you later.'

As expected, an article about the fire made the headlines: *Puits-Magdelon. Two teenagers burned alive in arson.*

Of the three photos illustrating the article, two were spread in width: the colors of the burning house were expertly retouched and enhanced. Border to border layout to enhanced the contrast, the photo of the charred remains with a subtle black and white effects. The third picture, cropped, showed the gendarmes and police van. One could figure Sylvain's back inside the van. On the foreground, there was the teenager, also shot from the back. He had one arm on the side and flipped a bird towards the photographer. Everything was on four columns:

'(...) Many clues suggest that it was an arson and a double homicide. Firefighters at the scene found the remains of gas cans and two charred bodies in a room locked from the outside.

'The victims were a young 19 year-old man and, a young 20 year-old woman. They were known at the gendarmerie of Puits-Magdelon, who had arrested them for the possession of cannabis. The amounts being less than three grams, they had been released. The brother and sister were from Guyana, and they had left home for about a year. No one knew why they had come to settle in Puits-Magdelon. Their family still lives in Guyana. The two victims went going to see them from time to time.

'The house, uninhabited for fifteen years, had attracted squatters, according to the inhabitants of the Avenue de la Gare. They were concerned about the many comings and goings they witnessed, especially at night. Young people, some being minors, occupied the house and made it their home or their headquarters.

'According to one of the neighbors, "We see them pass by with groceries. They seemed to live there, even in winter, but we didn't always see the same faces. Sometimes we could hear music all the time, music that sounded like jackhammers They also listened to rap: we can't always distinguish whether it was music or shouting matches from them. Nobody dared say anything since they were too afraid of revenge. Whenever there were police raids, there was never anyone. We wondered who warned them."

'Drug trafficking?

'A young 18 year-old man (pictured above) was arrested and taken into custody. The only son of a couple of butchers at Puits-Magdelon, Florent Marchadier no longer lives with his parents, with whom he was separated from

for two years. He was suspected of being the arsonist. In addition, he may be involved in drug trafficking far beyond the confines of Puits-Magdelon.

'The fire that killed the two young Guyanese could be a settling of accounts, as there often was in this business.'

The article lacked the macabre detail revealed by Gauthier: the victims were gagged and tied together with wire. The newspaper would sell less.

Before ascending the ladder with his cleaning equipment, he slipped a message under Maryse Beurdelet's door: 'Noise in the attic. No worries. I'm cleaning. S. Wolf.'

Once there, he closed the door behind him and placed his equipment on it: a way to be notified if someone came, one could never tell. Sylvain went face down and gently lifted the blanket he had placed on the hole in the floor during his last visit. Careful: no dust in Beurdelet! He took a look at the narrow opening, he waited. The bathroom light was on. Maryse Beurdelet finally made a brief appearance. She entered, placed or took something in a medicine cabinet, headed back out, leaving the light on. He had a good view of the washbasin surmounted by a large mirror and bath. He waited again. She came again, wrapped in her giant bathrobe. She removed it, revealing a transparent black nightie, leaving Sylvain stunned. It was one of those little feminine lingerie especially designed to titillate, when he had expected a thick cotton nightgown.

Sylvain found Maryse Beurdelet's body... quite beautiful. No... not beautiful, very beautiful. When she slid the nightgown over her head, her movements were graceful and moving. She revealed round breasts he would love to caress; light nipples he would take in his mouth; abundant brown fur in which he would dive into, plunge in for long, long time, while parting her creamy thighs slowly. Sylvain had palpitations and an erection that prevented from remaining flat on the hard ground. He was positioned slightly to the side and opened his fly. Now the woman was facing the mirror, and she poured hot water into the sink. He saw her back: the fine lines of which was emphasised by her wide hips; buttocks he would want to caress, squeeze and open. She pampered herself with a soapy washcloth: arms, armpits, breasts. He was transformed: the glove was him. She put one foot on the edge of the tub, and rubbed the glove back and forth between her legs. He rolled on his back, biting his lips, enjoying his thinking about the woman.

With a wave of an angry foot, Sylvain recovers the hole in the with the moth-eaten blanket. Armed with his broom, a shovel and a brush, he attacked the attic's dirt. He was angry with himself. 'Never again!' He swore to himself.

March. Mid-season. Spring! The gardeners rejoiced. But no, the meteorologists protested. Spring and autumn were only gardeners' inventions; winter and summer were the only two seasons!

Meanwhile, indifferent to these quarrels, buds grow.

Rue du Vau-L'Eau, along the blank walls of the courtyard, Sylvain planted: several species of ferns, golden privet, light green-white ivy, and forsythia flowers became bright accents in the dark courtyard. Once the risk of night frost was gone, he planned to remove a few more cobblestones in the yard, and plant summer-flowering shrubs. Previously, Sylvain asked for Salvignol's permission. 'The courtyard, I don't care about it, it's fine as it is. I have enough spending as it is,' she replied. But she still granted him permission, provided they do not contribute to the cost. Sylvain took from his savings from his sitting with Gadelorge. From the first planting, the court had become 'his' garden. Sylvain was in his dream world, and none of the tenants cared.

It has been three weeks since the fire and his delivery at Rue des Rouets. No news from Edgar Huggins – the better.

Since the first day of their collaboration, the Commissioner Gauthier ordered Sylvain to cut all contact with the tenants of the building. The situation was too risky for them. Just at that time, Odo Gadelorge decided to end the sittings to Sylvain's relief. Now Gadelorge fiddled with his picture. He warned Sylvain: 'I have never created a work so aesthetically mind-blowing. I will reveal it to you soon my dear, you have the premier. Have patience.' Sylvain brought him his regular postal parcels. They drank a glass of absinthe together – or two or three, as they were very small glasses. They did not need to talk.

As for Maryse Beurdelet, he regularly encountered her and she continued to ignore him, always no-touch. In Sylvain's mind, she was Maryse Beurdelet, not the woman in the bathroom. He now felt respect between them. He shares with her/them a secret, an 'unspeakable suffering' as Gadelorge would say. What violence had she suffered in her past to get there? Who violated Maryse Beurdelet? What unforgivable injury pushed her to want to blend in, to the point of disappearing?

In the attic, he repaired the glass in the skylight. Scraped, scoured, and revived the floor. He installed mousetraps and rat traps. And since he saw in others the signs of trouble, he felt a sense of solidarity. As a result, he plugged the floor of the hole with wood filler.

And so remained the case of Guylaine Monteil. She was rather of a tenacious nature. She has harassed since he went to her apartment to hang her paintings: flat boards with loud colors and geometric shapes. She insisted on inviting him to have lunch at her place: 'I want to thank you, Sylvain.' She called him Sylvain. Said Sylvain refused: 'No time.' She restarted like mischievous kid, 'I'm still waiting for lunch, Sylvain.' She sometimes tried the dinner invitation: 'One evening? It may be easier for you in the evening? Why not tonight? Or tomorrow night?' Sylvain invariably replied: 'Another time.' He had better refuse frankly, and this once and for all. He knew that. Why was it so hard to say no?

Today, Sylvain saw a familiar face spreads in the regional newspaper.

Headline: *Puits-Magdelon: another heinous crime at Avenue de la Gare*

The article recalled the previous episodes: '*A new crime took place a Avenue de la Gare, in the house next to the one that was burned three weeks ago; one in which two were killed: two young Guyanese voluntarily locked-in in the house (...)*

'*The alleged offender, Florent Marchadier, an 18 year-old Magdelonais is, as of this date, known to still be in custody.*

'*Yesterday, while returning from a late professional meeting around 22:00, Pierre-Louis Breuil, notary in Puits-Magdelon, found the body of his wife on the kitchen floor, naked and savagely slashed with multiple stab wounds. It was clear that the victim had been sexually abused. An autopsy has been ordered. The murder weapon - a kitchen knife belonging to Breuil - was planted in the womb of the victim. No forced entry and theft were found.*

'*According to our sources, many improbabilities in the alibi of Pierre-Louis Breuil led to his placement in custody.*

'*The victim, Mrs Sabine Breuil, was among the witnesses heard by the police at the time of the fire. The hypothesis of a link between the two cases was not excluded.*'

'She saw you. Too bad for her,' warned Huggins. His next victim should be Florent Marchadier, the other witness, the son of the market butcher. His detention should probably give him a reprieve, somehow unwittingly protect him.

Returning from the Press House, Sylvain found the headline cut out and folded in four under his door: 'Tonight 21:00, same place. Come with this newspaper page.'

01 on the mobile phone's keypad.

'Yes?' the Commissioner Gauthier responded instantly.

Sylvain spoke.

'21:00 at *Bon Bouilleur*. The message was written on the front page of today's newspaper with an article about...'

'Yes, yes. Don't panic. Keep me informed of the outcome of your appointment.'

Communication over.

'Don't panic, that's a good one,' spat Sylvain making his plants witness.

CHAPTER 5

'I'm satisfied with your services, Mr. Wolf. You have proven to me that you know how to keep your mouth shut. So we can move on to another stage. Is your ID card less than ten years old?'

'Yes.'

'Okay. The mission requires a round trip to Guyana. This time, you're not delivering. You'll be fetching goods.'

Sylvain wondered how he will be absent from his lodgings to go so far. New text for the sign hanging on the door of the lodge: 'The caretaker will be back soon: he went to Guyana.' The adventure was becoming as ridiculous as Edgar Huggins' Chicagoan character, with his Thirties getup in the middle of the Franco-French décor of *Bon Bouilleur*.

Tonight, Huggins did not come alone. A massive man sat next to him. Jar-head cut, and looked brutish in that narrow-minded way. Huggins took out of his pocket several notes of ten Euros. He counted aloud and spread them in a fan on the table.

'First of all, here are your first earnings: 200 Euros for your two deliveries.'

Sylvain dared not touch it. He knew it was called dirty money, and he did not know what kind of disease it transmitted.

'It's for you,' Huggins insisted.

His tone was obsequious, his arm gesture flying over the table surface was stupidly theatrical.

Edgar Huggins leaned over, his face too close for Sylvain's tastes.

'For the special operation that concerns us tonight, you earn double: 200 Euros in one go. What do you say to that, Mr. Wolf?'

In the absence of a reply, he continued.

'Tristan, here, will take you to the Orly airport. You will take a direct flight to Guyana. In order not to attract attention, bring luggage, as if you're leaving for a one week vacation. Not to mention it's hot there. In Cayenne, you will have two hours to spare to meet a certain Malcolm and follow his instructions to the letter. I said to the letter! Isn't that right, Mr. Wolf? Then direct return flight Cayenne-Paris. Tristan will be waiting at the airport to take you to Puits-Magdelon. Starting Thursday morning, you'll be back on Friday. You have tomorrow to notify Bérengère Salvignol of your absence: make up a family emergency. You tell anyone of Guyana, it won't make sense. Malcolm will address you and ask: "Would you like enjoy the small summer from March to visit Cayenne?" You will answer: "Of course, if it wasn't yet the rainy season." Then you will do ex-act-ly what he tells you, even if it surprises you. Ex-act-ly. Isn't that right, Mr. Wolf? Questions?'

Questions, Sylvain had many. But why? He still asked.

'A return trip on the same day, wouldn't that be suspicious?'

'Malcolm will explain. You will make up a story with him to justify your immediate return: your mother was dying or whatever. If necessary, Malcolm will pretend to be a friend to you and confirm your story. He knows many people in Cayenne. Here are your tickets. The return is an open ticket. You'll deal with it there. You'll leave Thursday morning at 05:00, at the church plaza of Puits-Magdelon. Tristan doesn't like to wait. Upon your return, he will send you further instructions. Bon voyage, Mr. Wolf.

Sylvain pockets the 200 Euros and airline tickets.

Tristan was the type of human with the head of a bear. Same round eyes close for a long snout, and even growls when a motorist had the audacity of attempting to overtake him. So far, none have succeeded. Whether they were trying it in advance or just stick their car behind his, they were all faked out. He often had his eyes on his mirrors. Upon seeing a car on the left lane, he waited the last moment to disengage and cut him off, dropping his many horses. His grunts were more threatening when he saw a woman driving: he allowed her to start overtaking him, until the two cars were side by side and at that moment, vrooom, he thoroughly accelerated and turned in a sudden swerve. Then he looks at the effect obtained in the mirror with the smile of a dominant male.

The car was a great recent Mercedes sedan, equipped with leather seats and overloaded with gadgets which Sylvain knew nothing about, all in a concert of continuous beeping. Tristan quickly drove, he concentrated, he never said a word. He ignored Sylvain's existence whose only hope of standing out would be to go jumping into the middle of the road – and he wasn't even sure of it! Tristan would be able to run him over just to keep his lead. They drove for three hours. Orly was not far off.

Sylvain was vexed: highway and another highway yet, all throughout the journey. At daybreak, he found a landscape of empty fields, so distant that the villages seemed to belong to another world, with stink ring roads, and a show of slopes where vegetation was all wrong. When they stopped at a rest area, he touched the trees to make sure it was not a scene set there to entertain motorists.

Car-nature match: 40 million against 1.

Following the trip – because it certainly looked like one – was no more attractive. They arrive at Orly with three hours in advance. Tristan stopped the car with the engine running and kept his hands on the wheel, looking steadfastly before him. Sylvain understood that he will not accompany him any further.

He had never seen an airport, and finally here was one. The space was so vast that it made him dizzy and wobbly while walking. Human traffic was worse than a train station, maybe because travelers were more worried. They looked tense – and Sylvain was with them – when they scanned the multitude of signs overloaded with arrows, symbols, letters, numbers... There were too many or not enough, making his dizziness worse. The loud speakers may have calm announcements, but they sometimes triggered crowd movements, which resembled panic attacks. Such cosmopolitan concentration created an exotic atmosphere, very frightening for Sylvain Wolf of Puits-Magdelon.

All aboard? Welcome on board? Why did aviation she borrowed the terms of the navy? It could make an effort to create its own language.

Eight hours of dozing and boredom. So this was an airplane. He tried to escape in his dreams, but the environment was not appropriate. He sat between two sweaty people, and the promiscuity disturbed him.

Sylvain wondered if the henchmen of the Commissioner Gauthier accompanied him in this journey. When he told him he was leaving or Guyana, he showed no surprise. He was content to say, 'Be careful, you're playing in the big leagues. Call me when you get back.'

Cayenne. Rochambeau Airport. Sylvain was now watching his backpack on the treadmill luggage. A hand was on his shoulder. He turned with an accelerated movement, in an adrenaline rush and discovered a head without hair, no eyebrows – a man who looks as friendly as Tristan. The man recited his long password, Sylvain followed his cue. It was Malcolm. His Mehari, hand-painted in khaki, was a curious mish-mash of spare parts. It rolled along. It left the county, engaged a forest track and jolted in the ruts of a barely passable transect before stopping in the forest.

Malcolm took off his jacket. With infinite care, he spread it on Sylvain's knee and tore lining. Many small pouches the size of thimbles emerged. They contained a white substance.

'You're going to swallow those. There are fifty. They're condoms. Watch out, they're fragile. If you burst them, you'll burst too. When you get home from here, you'll shit to get them back. Come on, swallow.'

Malcolm pulled out a gun from the waistband of his pants, then pointed them between the pouches and Sylvain's mouth.

'Step on it, you got a plane to catch.'

Sylvain was exhausted. He will put an end to this crazy story. For good. 'If this man shoots me in the head, the better!' Sudden death, without suffering. This was an opportunity to end this life. He has seen enough. A lone wolf cannot become the plaything of a Huggins and a Gauthier. Enough was enough.

'Step on it, I said!'

Around, from the canopy to the woods, many animals cried out to draw Sylvain's attention and they put their whole heart into it. Finally, he listened. Finally, he noted the tropical vegetation that was quick to show off all its glory. Finally, it returned to earth He will live a little – wildlife claimed victory.

He swallowed one cocaine-filled condom at a time. He drew it out, and drew it out long. He stuffed a sachet, swallowed, felt an uncomfortable pain in his esophagus. He did it again – fifty times.

Back to Cayenne.

'I'll stay here until your boarding. If ever there's an ass who asks you if you travel back and forth for 14000 kilometers in one day, tell them that you just learned that your wife's giving birth three months in advance, and she might die. The hospital wants you to sign a release to sacrifice the kid and save the mother. If the mess with you,' said Malcolm, 'give me a sign.'

Suddenly, it was chaos. A man just before Sylvain in the passenger queue was dragged out by the police. He escaped them, and knocked over two people in the process. Shrill cries rose in the frightened crowd. Police officers were popping up everywhere and surrounded him. The fugitive was arrested. It was a muscular guy who fought to the end. Four was needed to neutralize him. Passengers were anxious – two were knocked over and complained of being injured – it was a mess. Finally, everyone was asked to hurry. Sylvain crossed safely through the turbulence zone, and crosses to the entrance to the departure lounge. Nobody asked why he was to return two hours after his arrival.

He slept intermittently during the painful return trip. Upon Malcolm's advice, he pretended to eat the rata pâlichon in his tray and discreetly emptied it into a plastic bag, and then went to the toilet. 'No eating, no drinking. Don't you dare to puke! Understand? Watch out that no one sees you. Those who track the mules, a passenger who doesn't eat is suspicious.' said Malcolm before his departure.

The thought that his stomach was weighed down by fifty pouches of latex hurt. Cramps attacked his belly. It could be that he would expel his cargo in the plane's bathroom.

The next morning, Paris-Orly airport, finally.

The police there, too, were monopolized by a show of a big arrest. Hand luggage was ripped under the nose of a terrified guy who screamed and cried, 'It's not mine! It's not mine! Someone put it all in my bag!' The other passengers, including Sylvain, went through inspection faster than expected.

Among the joyful faces who were anxiously awaiting relatives, was Tristan's expressionless muzzle. Sylvain was almost glad to see him. All he wanted was to quickly go back to the stable – and Tristan did it very well, at full speed in a convertible devilishly dashing Aston Martin coupe.

Once arrived at the church of Puits-Magdelon, Tristan spoke – so he knew how to, after all.

'You'll put on these suppositories. It's laxative. You'll see, it's fast. I'll come to your place. And I will stay until you give me the merchandise. Go there first. I'll be there.

In other circumstances, Sylvain could never relieve an explosive bowel movement in the presence of a stranger sitting nearby. But in the present situation, his energy was focused on one goal: get rid of Tristan and ignoble pouches as quickly as possible. He heared them fall down with muffled sounds in the bucket upon which he was folded in half. He was shaken by painful contractions triggered by the powerful laxative. When he cleaned the pouches under the faucet to count, thirty-one were missing. He would cry as he was exhausted. Several hours and suppositories later, fifty condoms were intact, and Tristan emerges with his junk.

On the coffee table Sylvain twenty ten Euro notes were arranged in a fan.

After listening to Sylvain's story, Commissioner Gauthier spoke in turn.

'You have to enter the world of drug couriers. They're called "mules" because they're loaded with drugs. And also "bucks" when they ingest coke. Some die. If a bag of pure cocaine - it's called an "egg" - breaks under the effect of gastric fluid, intoxication is massive and often fatal. There were also cases of bowel obstruction. Not to mention those who have had their bellies opened, pressed by bosses to get their merchandise. For routing via the human body, dealers constantly think up new tricks. For example, yellow capsules of the "Kinder egg", well known to children, were sometimes used: they were waterproof and were resistant to gastric juices. They also have the right shape to be inserted and concealed in the anus. Mules are volunteers. The vast majority are people from very poor places, and carefully selected by traffickers. Before accepting applications, these unscrupulous individuals identify families. And threaten the worst paybacks to ensure the silence of the passer when stopped by the police. As I said, the traffickers' imagination was unlimited. Cocaine hidden in hollowed fruits and vegetables, cans, toothpaste tubes, tourist trinkets, prostheses and medical plasters, etc. Hair wasn't spared either - in buns or dreadlocks, or frames and lenses of spectacles had compounds of cocaine. Chemical methods abound. Cocaine was converted into an odorless substance to fool dogs, then restored into its original form with solvents or ether. There were even suitcases of mixed plastic and cocaine. The mixture masked the smell of the drugs. In the end, a chemist separates the molecules to get cocaine, knowing that there will be traces of toxic plastic. The sniffer will get it up the nose. For a delivery of a larger scale, a method was provided for chemically transforming cocaine into Plexiglas. Not bad when it comes to being undetected. Traffic through the human body was juicy, even if it limited the amount. To give you an idea: a mule, who ingested a kilo of cocaine in the form of a hundred eggs, carried enough to make 20,000 doses. The market value was estimated at 1.2 million at the time. The mule was busted: police attention was attracted because she was traveling without luggage. She confessed that she should have hit 4,000 Euros for transport. Traffickers sometimes use simple tourists, who were tempted by amounts ranging from 1,000 to 3,000 Euros for a transport. Other transport drugs without their knowledge hidden in their luggage, and were greeted on arrival by dealers who were far from friendly. Moreover, the scenes that you at Cayenne and Orly airports are common. As a diversion, traffickers willingly sacrifice one or two of their smugglers. They load them with cannabis, for example, then do so as they'll be nabbed. During that time, another mule passes by with his cocaine in the stomach, a much higher value. This was what has happened to you, you were the mule "to cover." The two other smugglers didn't know they were condemned in advance. That's it. This is a brief overview, and only for cocaine. For it was then that traffic primarily interested Edgar Huggins. From cocaine base, he also manufacture crack to reach those who do not have the means to buy coke. Generally to the younger ones. And he reserves cannabis to attract even younger people. As for ecstasy, it was used not only for its traffic in France, he exports it. It was better that you were summarily aware of the mysteries of this environment. Too naïve, and it could've lead to your loss. You're not one of the volunteer mules but Huggins found a good way to pressure you: he made you fear losing your job. And it worked. From what you have told me, he also threatened to torture you. I urge you to believe him. Edgar Huggins has a strategy with you. Unlike some smugglers, you were paid, little by little. All the better to keep you. Huggins knows you were poor, so he gives you the taste for money, he makes you addicted. For now, he pays you in modest sums. With 100 or 200 Euros, you get paid at the rate of mules from South American slums. You might also get 1,000 to 3,000 Euros per transit. To hold you, it will go on the crescendo. You're on your warm-up period. He will definitely use you in a larger operation. Get ready.'

'No. It's over. I don't want to anymore.'

Downtime. Sylvain's left ear was hot under the prolonged contact of the mobile phone. He hanged to the right just in time to relieve the cramps on his left arm.

'You cannot refuse, you won't have a choice,' resumed Commissioner Gauthier in a neutral voice.

'I have the choice to prefer to die right away.'

New downtime.

'I ask you to listen to me carefully, Mr. Wolf. Reassembling the Huggins industry just to dismantle the network is a huge operation. We were on the spot for years. We have never been so close to reaching the goal and, shit, this really is not the time to chicken out. Trust me, not only you will soon be rid of this dirty business, but you will also be rewarded for your services. Very handsomely. OK?'

'I'm not interested.'

'So, what do we do? Do I arrest you right away for your involvement in drug trafficking? You also have another charge: arson, for example. OK? I can also, if you prefer, by dig up a third one: the murder of Josée Nadar.'

Unexpected irruption of Nadar. Commissioner Gauthier came strongly. He kept the Nadar card in his sleeve and waited for the right time to bring it down. Did he know something? Was he bluffing? Regardless, Sylvain did not bend.

'Do what you want, Commissioner. I don't care.'

He heard nothing, as if Gauthier had hung up. By the way, could one also say 'hang up' for a mobile phone without the handset? He was beginning to ask this crucial question when the Commissioner took the floor.

'You're shaken by your experience and you're still in shock. We'll clear this up tomorrow. Call me in the morning. Okay?'

'Yes.'

Sylvain answered the call of its plants, which needed to be reassured, 'But yes, you are as beautiful as your Guyanese cousins.'

Someone drummed on the door of the lodge, it was not a dream. Sylvain took the time to emerge from a sleep of several hours. He slept all afternoon.

A radiant Gadelorge waited at the door. He changed his hairstyle. Parted in the middle separated black-dyed hair, bobbed. White regrowth draw a path of three centimeters wide at the top of his skull.

He was impatiently hopping.

'Come see your portrait!' He begged, hands clasped.

Without delay, he climbed the stairs trumpeting:

'Hurry up, my dear! You are the first to see it, as promised.'

Odon Gadelorge laid the painting on an easel, covered with a white sheet. The bottle of absinthe and two small glasses (never washed) sat expectant on the trestle table.

'Ready, Mr Wolf?' demanded Gadelorge smiling, pretending to tug at a corner of the sheet.

Sylvain played the game: he formally approach the easel, and crossed his arms and stood straight, arched back, staring ahead.

'Ready.'

Odon Gadelorge undressed his work with loving gestures. The two friends shared a long moment of contemplation. The capture work hit hard, especially with the rendering of light. The single source, the window with the low winter glow, was insufficient to illuminate the entire room. Everything was dark, save for the reflections on the white shirt of the seated figure. His face turned to the daylight appeared in a partially shaded halo, half-lighted. His bare shoulder drew the eye to light colors, a little blurred. His silhouette blended with the decor in earth tones with hints of black. On the whole picture, the artist played with many varieties of ochres. Here and there, discrete yellow gold touches highlighted contours hidden at first sight. His posture, his expression, while the character emanated an ineffable sadness. Sylvain burst into tears. Odon Gadelorge took him in his arms, and waited for the end of last sob to whisper.

'Your tears, Sylvain, is the greatest compliment.' It was the first time he called him Sylvain.

It had been ten days since he called the Commissioner Gauthier back, as agreed.

'Shall we continue?'

'We'll continue.'

They did not say anything more.

Despite the precautions – avoiding relationships with tenants Huggins' case was ongoing – Sylvain relented to the assaults of Guylaine Monteil. He accepted her invitation to dinner.

The evening began coolly.

'Are you okay that we are on familiar terms?' immediately requested a joyful Guylaine.

'No, I'm not.'

She seemed very upset. There was an unease in the air.

'I'll get something in the kitchen,' she announced as a diversion.

She regained her composure when she returned with a tray of canapés rillettes. Exhilarated, she opened the bottle of Bordeaux brought by Sylvain and filled the glasses.

'Chin!'

'Chin.'

'I made a quiche with tuna, mixed salad and a chocolate mousse for dessert. You like them?'

'Yes.'

Sylvain wonders how he will spend the whole evening with this stranger. He had nothing to say. What was he doing here?

The dinner was very good. He enjoyed home cooking. Guylaine recounted her years of life on earth through a series of anecdotes that all beginning with the same words: 'I'll never understand what happened to me that day...' She never shut up.

The salad finished, she went into the kitchen without interrupting their chatter and brought a second bottle of wine with a well-made, well chosen camembert. Sylvain drank little. He witnessed Guylaine Monteil's transformation. Her chubby cheeks went from pink to deep red, her chatter accelerated. She was cheerful and tipsy, then more and more drunk. Finally, there was an intermission.

'Be right back. Above all, don't move.'

Sylvain was in a hurry to go but do not dare to just sit there, when they have not even finished dinner. There remained the chocolate mousse.

From the bedroom, rose the first notes of the ever famous hit song of the Seventies: Lady Marmalade. Guylaine entered, wearing a bright pink skirt and a purple blouse with frills. A black lace shawl was thrown over her shoulders. She stuck her short hair with gel and teased them into steep spikes. She looked like a wet electrocuted cat if one had asked Sylvain. Rhythmically, she into a strip of her own: she swirled the shawl around her with gestures that she probably found sensual, lingering over each button of her blouse. When the chorus arrives, she wrapped the shawl around and sung a duet with Patti LaBelle.

Voulez-vous coucher avec moi, ce soir

Voulez-vous coucher avec moi

Of course Sylvain would like sleep with her; a voluptuous woman. But there was an insurmountable obstacle on the lower floor: a listening Edgar Huggins, like a retriever, tail and ears erect.

Sylvain heard himself say, 'I'm not feeling so well, I have a fever. I'm going home. Sorry and thank you for... uh... the very good dinner.'

Guylaine was so wasted she heard nothing. She continued to twirl.

Voulez-vous coucher avec moi, ce soir

Voulez-vous coucher avec moi

Finale: she collapsed on the carpet, face down, arms outstretched. Her pink skirt raised on a nice piece of ass swallowing a G-string. Suddenly, her body was twitching: it was laughter. He took the opportunity to slip away.

It was exciting, Sylvain admitted. Yes, of course. But in his mind, that place was taken; Maryse Beurdelet was not forgotten. Guylaine Monteil can go get dressed.

A skeleton of a market stroller – Sylvain had exhumed it from his cubbyhole. He used it to carry the bags of potting soil purchased at the garden center;

plants as well. April began in sweetness, he wanted to go see the new plant nursery at the market. His cookie jar contained 280 Euros of what remained from the sessions with Gadelorge, and 400 Euros from Huggins' deliveries. Such fun.

The more he approached the market, the more he could smell something unusual in the atmosphere. Gossip was more animated and voices over heated. Jeannot Marchadier's deli stand was covered with a tarpaulin. A paper was stuck on it: 'Closed for family reasons.' Sylvain walked through painstakingly talkative groups. The plant nursery side was even agitated. He would have liked to have more serenity to choose his plants.

Gossip around him related exclusively to Florent Marchadier, son of the butcher, 'It appears that his two cellmates saw nothing, heard nothing. You bet! A guy who hangs himself makes some noise! I believe not a word. This was not a suicide, he was murdered, yes! In this place, it's not all choir boys. They were often seen on TV. Besides, that's where they take their ideas, all these young people. By trying to be like the Yanks. Why, if my kid was on drugs, I'll see it right away. How was it that his parents were not aware? And his father, so friendly and cheerful. Oh, he Florent played him a fool! He paid with his life, as we say. Such is the time we live in now!'

Huggins said, Huggins did: he deleted the second witness of Avenue de la Gare. The other was that Sabine Breuil murdered with knives. Her husband, Pierre-Louis Breuil was still languishing in custody for a crime he probably did not commit.

Sylvain brought neither plants nor newspapers. He left. He did not want to find out more.

A plastic bag was placed on the doormat of his box. It contained a chocolate mousse ramekin and a note: 'Sylvain. I was really drunk last night. I hope we'll meet again. See you soon? Guylaine.'

'Hello, yes?'

'Tomorrow I'm going to Anvers. A return day trip,' recited Sylvain.

'By what means of transportation?'

'Tristan will take me to Paris by car, then I take the train. No tickets reserved for either trip. It seems that there are connecting trains between Paris and Anvers every hour. My rendezvous is inside the Anvers train station. When I return, Tristan will be waiting for me at Gare du Nord.'

'This is all you know?'

'Yes. Huggins gave me 200 Euros to buy train tickets and a disposable phone to communicate with Tristan.'

'He's paying you how much?'

'Three times more than the trip to Guyana: 600 Euros.'

'Mr Wolf?'

'Yes.'

'Don't forget our last discussion. I always keep my promises. Call me as soon as you come home.'

What promise did Commissioner Gauthier speak of? Sylvain questioned. He made two: an immediate arrest, a big paycheck.

Sylvain had an old uncle in Paris, with a serious illness. He refused to go to hospital. He was therefore treated at home. A nurse was on site 24 hours. This uncle – the was the brother of his father – considered Sylvain as his son. He welcomed him home after the death of his parents until his departure for military service. Sylvain loved him, was very attached him and... there was not one word of truth! Fortunately, the owner swallowed the story at the time of his departure in Guyana. 'Go see him. Keep me posted. Also, inform the tenants,' she said in an almost soft voice. She even added, 'Don't be away too often or too long. And continue to do your sixty hours of work per month.'

Sylvain used the disposable mobile to leave a message on Salvignol's answering machine: 'My uncle called me. I'm returning to Paris tomorrow. I'll return in the evening.'

It was not the muddy Volvo station wagon, the large luxury Mercedes sedan coupe, nor the convertible Aston Martin. It was a nervous city car, a last generation Mini Cooper. Tristan had to have chosen to best slalom in the streets of the capital. As soon as the bouncing car – apparently dolled by maniac – engaged the peripheral road, Tristan's bears grunts were laced with commentary: 'Move, you fat seal... Take it in the ass, you cod ... fuck off, bitch, you're as ugly as your junk!' His flowery language worsened once he reached Boulevard

Barbès. He yelled, windows down. But he forgot that a drunk Parisian driver was not the type to let a Magdelonais piss him off. Tristan puts the pedal to the metal, and was still furious. In the middle of the dizzying din his shouting, they do no more than a cry of the ant deep in the jungle. They approach Gare du Nord. On the Boulevard de Magenta, pedestrians, cyclists, bus drivers and motorists engage in a fight to the death. Pollution will be responsible for ending the survivors.

Sylvain knew Paris for having lived many years there at a time when every neighborhood had its village life. In addition, the Parisians had a sense of belonging to their district, which was shared community. He did not know what happened to the Paris of today, but he found the Parisians filthy.

From Gare du Nord to the Antwerpen-Centraal station, the journey time was two hours. Sylvain absorbed in reading a series, *Rustica*. On the seat next to him, a traveler killed boredom by biting his nails and dozing off. He rushed to start the conversation when Sylvain closed his magazine.

'You know Antwerpen?'

'No.'

'So you've never seen the station!'

'No.'

'You'll be blown away!' he raced with a pronounced Belgian accent. 'It's the fourth most beautiful station in the world! It was built between 1895 and 1905. The recent renovation of the historic building was a beauty. Above all, I implore you, take your time to admire it. You will first be struck by the quality and color of the Vinalmont Stone. You know? It was a limestone from

Meuse which takes a light-gray patina with age. You will lose your mind overt the profusion of columns from different styles: Doric, Tuscan, Ionic, Corinthian. You can caress twenty marbles of various origins. Kneel to contemplate the floor of the great hall. Then look up the beautiful structures in iron and glass that let in daylight and sunlight. Above the hall, the dome rises to 75 meters high! You will fall over backwards. You will be stunned by the majesty of the huge dome. The canopy soars 45 meters above the tracks, featuring gorgeous raspberry tones – yes, I said 'raspberry'. You will be dazzled by the perfection of the details of this work of art. And that's not all – a masterpiece will leave you amazed: a railway viaduct! It's still of its time, completely restored. I hope this brief encounter will give a lasting memory. Me, you will forget me, of course, but your feelings, they will remain forever imprinted in your memory.'

This may be Odon Gadelorge's Belgian cousin, thought Sylvain – like in talk and enthusiasm.

The cousin subsided by thoroughly cleaning the lenses of his glasses.

'I am a businessman. I travel a lot. As much as possible, preferably I take the train. If you knew how I saturated the disastrous spectacle of identical airports. The architects were missing artists. They were replaced by soulless technical offices that build quickly and cheaply with cold and shoddy materials. And you? What were you doing in life?'

Sylvain hesitated. Businessman? He, too, was a businessman. That was exactly what he was doing.

'I am a caretaker.'

'Oh, how I envy you,' sighed the businessman suddenly overwhelmed. 'What if we swapped lives?'

Final station.

His companion told him that the Anvers train station was one of the four most beautiful in the world. Having no knowledge of the other three, Sylvain immediately assigned it the first place. He never imagined he would one day be receptive to railway architecture.

It was a pity that so many people were in that cathedral. He would have liked to be alone and absorb its beauty. Sylvain felt very small, but strangely, he was not overwhelmed by the enormity of the place. Proportions, lines and volumes came together to give the impression of a tamed space. Only an artist of the 1900s, could explain the secret in making a work that can please him without knowing why. Sylvain could see Odon Gadelorge swooning in front of his easel. 'An aesthetically overwhelming work,' he said. If he saw the Anvers train station, he would probably say the same thing.

He had an appointment in the large hall with a so-called Jasper, supposedly disabled. He would be in a wheelchair and the address at the foot of the stone staircase (Vinalmont?) which seemed to have more balusters than stairs. In pacing, Sylvain afraid of dirtying it, hardly dared to touch his soles on the marble floor. The colors would appeal to Gadelorge: white, light gray, ocher, black.

'What if we came back here together, Odo and I?'

He had no time to think too long. Jasper arrived as expected in a wheelchair, a travel bag on his lap. His legs were completely atrophied, disability was far from fake. The password was easier than usual: 'Hi buddy, I'm glad to see you. 'And Sylvain replied: 'Likewise, Jasper.'

However, the following was unexpected:

'Would you come with me to the bathroom? I need help to pee.'

They go in one of two symmetrical arched quadrants located under the monumental staircase and entered together in the toilet for the disabled. Sylvain was very anxious when Jasper opened his travel bag.

'Tell Tristan that it went well: 15 pounds in 15 bags in heat-sealed plastic. Take them in your backpack. After we're out of the bathroom together, you push my chair up to the exit and we part as if we were friends.'

He had nothing to swallow! Sylvain's relief brought tears to his eyes.

As they crossed the lobby, Jasper motioned for him to stop and muttered:

'Over there, there's a guy who's looking at us strangely. I don't like that at all! Make a call to Tristan. Ask him what you should do.'

The 'yeah?' from Tristan was heard through the green disposable phone. The exchange lasted barely a minute.

'Tristan said he shouldn't I take the train immediately,' Sylvain announced after hanging up.' We will first walk together to the zoo which is right next to the train station. We'll call him back in half an hour.

'What? He's mad! You're sure?

'Yes.'

'Shit, shit. Shit shit shit!'

Sylvain, as for himself, was inwardly pleased to have the opportunity to go to the zoo.

They did not see the man with the bizarre look approaching. He walked with small jerky steps beside the chair Jasper leaned towards him and, in a barely audible voice, he whispered

'For 40 Euros, I'll go to the toilet with you.'

'Another time. For today, that's enough.' replied Jasper without showing the slightest surprise.

The other did not insist. Jasper watched him until he disappeared into the crowd, then suddenly agitated, shakes Sylvain arm.

'Call Tristan again, quickly! Tell him it was only a whore.'

With Tristan's agreement, the two men stayed there and left on a role play: 'Bye man!' and 'See you soon!'

The train to Paris came in forty minutes. Sylvain had the time to take a walk in the zoo of the park, the trees of which he already saw out of the station. 15 kilos of cocaine weighed all their weight in his backpack to remind him, gently but firmly, that this was not the time.

Oh alright.

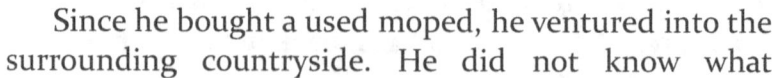

Since he bought a used moped, he ventured into the surrounding countryside. He did not know what

euphoria was. Well: he finally experienced it. He did not believe in freedom. Well: he finally felt it. They were only feelings, of course, it did not mean that they existed.

The first time he discovered the forest near Puits-Magdelon, he acknowledged his element as if it included a natural environment designed specifically for him. 'Look, that's the wolf!' Shouted his friends from kindergarten to tease, unaware that they were being cruel. Finally, they may be right.

At first, he stalked the forest's trails marks of Tom Thumb to find his way. It soon became useless. Although the forest was extensive, he was never lost: it was his territory, he was its host, they know each other.

Under the terms of his employment contract, Salvignol allowed him to be gone for four hours a day. He often spent his time in the forest. Not today, however, because he had to go to the bookstore. The approach intimidated him – he passed by several times before the window, not daring to enter – but the desire to find a book on trees was stronger than anything.

He chose the largest bookstore in Puits-Magdelon. Nice surprise, the atmosphere reassured immediately. There, everybody minded their own business. The trader respected the client, who can snoop around, read, take their time. The section, easy to find, was called 'Nature, animals, gardening.' Sylvain stayed there for over an hour and was resigned to select three books among others: *Guide to European Trees*, *Wild Plants*, *Forever Trees*.

'For the loyalty card, under whose name should I put it under?' asked the bookseller.

'Sylvain Wolf.'

'W-o-l-f. Like a wolf?

'…'

'Huh?'

'Yes. Like a wolf.'

He still strolled about the bookstore when female voice whispered in his ear.

'I'll wait outside.'

It was Marie-Jeanne Languerrand.

There was nothing much that made Sylvain drop from the highest branch of the tree where his dreams had perched upon. The famous bigot of Puits-Magdelon, equally famous deceased mayor's sister, waited in effect on the opposite sidewalk, all in black under a black umbrella. Sylvain could see her well in the role of headmistress of a boarding school for girls in the Sixties.

'Come with me,' she said.

'To where?'

'You'll see.'

Rain upset him; not for himself but for his books. Sylvain protected them as well as he can by keeping them hidden under his jacket. They borrowed a maze of streets, one behind the other on too narrow and sloping pavements, beyond the last houses of the city. It opened into a vacant lot behind the industrial area, the famous industrial zone where Sylvain followed Edgar Huggins the first time.

High walls of gray stone surrounded a wood which the end could not be seen. They stop in front of a vaulted porch, and Marie-Jeanne Languerrand whispered a password into the intercom. With a clack, the studded wooden door opened. At the end of a path lined with flowering chestnuts, two towers flanked a castle with a facade of brick and stone. Rich meadows made horses dream, the heads of which exceed a dozen boxes in a lengthy stable. Paths sunk under large trees that crowded against each other.

A man received them, giving Sylvain a déjà vu. He had an uncanny resemblance to Tristan albeit more puny. He wore the same striped jacket as Nestor in *The Adventures of Tintin*, and made a lot of fuss to take Languerrand's coat and umbrella. Sylvain would not let go his books, but Nestor withdrew his authority.

'Please be seated. The master will here soon,' he solemnly announced.

They waited in a lounge with the flashy decor. Sylvain expected Huggins to appear (if the announced 'master' was him) wearing a smoking jacket in burgundy satin with a bow tie to match.

He entered into launching a condescending 'Stay seated.' It was certainly Huggins. His disguise was more refined than usual three-piece anthracite suit, white carnation in his buttonhole, big tie, white spats, white Borsalino with a black ribbon. This was the first time that Sylvain had seen him in a well-lighted room. His quickdraw Italian Mafioso of the last century look did not jive with his mixed Indian look. Native Americans – their culture, their expertise, their way of life – had always attracted Sylvain; save for that guy.

Three intense black setters tumbled into the lounge. Their coats had tan markings of a rich chestnut red, two of which sat neatly over their eyes – Gadelorge's colors. One of the three was a puppy which rushed to Sylvain and hopped to climb on his lap.

'Here, Goodboy!' Huggins ordered.

The puppy wanted to play and continued to make leaps, yelping. Sylvain whispered, 'Gently, Goodboy, gently.' Huggins brandished a whip and gave a second order.

'Goodboy, heel!'

Upon seeing the whip, Goodboy joined his master and sat by casting miserable a glance towards Sylvain.

Huggins turned to Marie-Jeanne Languerrand.

'Thank you Marie-Jeanne. You can leave us now.'

The woman in black withdrew, as constipated as Beurdelet on her bad hair days.

'If you are here tonight, Mr. Wolf, consider it as a kind of induction to a small circle. Only a chosen few were aware of my home. We can say that you quickly rose through the ranks. Keep it up. First, stop procrastinating. You understand, I suppose, that you are participating in a drug trafficking?'

'Yes.'

'The mission that I wish to assign to you is different from the previous ones. I have a problem to solve with one of my couriers. Octavo is a Franco-Brazilian man who lives in Paris. Unknown to the police, he's in the food business as a cover. He has a share of my trusted men. Or he would, it seems, organized a side-traffic of his own. I need to check on him. That's what you'll do: go to Paris, you meet Octavo as planned, and you get my merchandise. Until then, it's business as usual. Then you ask him where you can get crack for your personal use, specifying that you need a lot. Do not, at any account, go out and follow him wherever. If he agrees to give you 100 grams, it'll be enough evidence to bring him down on the spot. You will have a gun. Be the first to shoot, because he's probably armed. Any questions, Mr Wolf?'

'I don't know how to use a gun.'

'Tristan will teach you. For all the details, go see him. He will meet you tomorrow night at 21:00 next to the church of Puits-Magdelon. You will receive 800 Euros. Zero Euros if Octavo escapes you. In the latter case, we will make further decisions upon your return. Isn't that right, Mr. Wolf?'

Huggins slipped his hand under his desk and probably rang a bell probably because Nestor appeared instantly. Suddenly awakened, Goodboy emerged from his puppy dreams, stumbled to Sylvain and nibbled down his pants.

'Martial will escort you, Mr Wolf. Hold On, one more thing: if you manage this double operation, Goodboy's yours. He's a three month old Gordon setter. You want him?'

Sylvain nodded.

Over the phone, Gauthier did not interrupt Sylvain's report, and said coldly.

'If you kill this Octavo, it will be self-defense. Don't get lost in your emotions. It's him or you.'

'Are the police continuing to protect me?'

'Of course! More than ever! Proper police protection is unobtrusive. It's normal that you don't see them. We're ready to intervene in the case of absolute necessity. Okay?'

'What, for example, would be a case of absolute necessity?'

'Be content to hope that there hasn't been any yet. Carry on with your work, you're very effective. We're getting much closer. Stay cautious. And call me when you get back.'

Sylvain put down his exclusive mobile for Gauthier and took the green disposable phone. Then as he thought of leaving a message Salvignol answered.

'Hello?'

'It's Sylvain Wolf. I leave tomorrow evening for Paris to see my uncle. I'll return in the morning.'

'Good. Leave a note on your office door to notify tenants.'

'Yes, as usual. Uh … I wanted to say something else.'

'Well?'

'Would you allow me to have a dog?'

'Oh my! Usually, no, I don't allow it. It may bark and disturb the tenants.'

'If he bothers anyone, I won't keep him.'

'I'm warning you: I will not tolerate any complaints. Take your dog, but be ready to rid of him soon as the first problem comes up. Understand?'

Yes, Sylvain has understood. If necessary, he will go live elsewhere with Goodboy. So much for the lodge. Before leaving, he will offer his plants Odon Gadelorge.

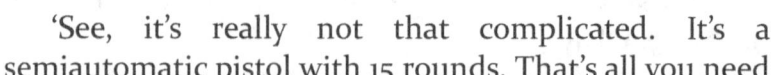

'See, it's really not that complicated. It's a semiautomatic pistol with 15 rounds. That's all you need to know. You'll throw it into the Seine along with Octavo's body. Your appointment's at 02:00 at the tip of Ile de la Cité. Square du Vert-Galant is closed at night. You'll take the longer road and go to the tip of the dock. You know where that is?'

'Yes, I see where it is.'

'I'll put you in front of the La Samaritaine and you continue on foot. Octavo will say: "At this hour, the Pont-Neuf cruisers don't sail." You'll answer: "The swans are quieter." Call me when you're done and I'll tell you where I'll pick you up to take you back.'

Sylvain was ten minutes early. It rained enough to deter the night owls who come walking here and there. However, there were a lot of rustling in the square. Sylvain hoped it was not a den of the homeless. The presence of witnesses would force him to drop everything. By his observing, he made out little eyes blinking in the darkness. There were many, they were brown rats, sewer rats, as they were called by Parisians. He would have liked to look closer but someone came to him.

'At this hour, the Pont-Neuf cruisers don't sail,' said a singsong voice.

The password was correct, it was Octavo. Sylvain replied.

'The rrr ... swans are quieter.'

He barely caught himself, he almost replaced the swans by rats.

'Everything is. There's no lizard,' said Octavo. He opened a sports bag, the flaming light of a lighter saw more heat-sealed plastic bags, like those of the Anvers train station. Others were transparent pockets containing yellowish pebbles species.

Thoughts were racing very fast in Sylvain's head, 'I won't kill him. I'll tell him that Huggins is aware of his side-traffic. Then, I'll make believe Huggins that I killed him.'

'Well, I'll leave the bag. Good night,' said Octavo.

'Wait. I have a question. You know where I can find crack for myself?'

'For you? You don't look like...'

'It takes a lot.'

'And, in your little head, was how many is 'a lot'?'

'100 grams.'

Octavo approached, hands on his hips. Sylvain felt sweat dripping between his shoulder blades.

'Hey asshole! Either you're stupid, or you think I'm stupid. Who do you work for?'

A movement of Octavo's arm to his hip pocket triggered the same gesture from Sylvain, much more vividly: he shot three bullets randomly at close range in Octavo's belly, which made the latter open his mouth and his eyes all wide, and he collapsed. He curled up on the floor. Flowing blood was diluted by the rain that continued to fall abundantly. Octavo was still alive. Sylvain hesitated to end him. He had already fired three shots, and the sound should have been heard far as the river accentuated the echo of the detonation.

Octavo was dying, then he died. Sylvain pushed the body in the slope of the platform. Splash. He threw the gun away. Splash. The Seine had seen others.

The raw green mobile worked well enough under the curtain of rain.

'I'll be waiting near the Vélib' station at Rue de l'Arbre Sec,' said Tristan, clipped.

Crossing the Pont Neuf, Sylvain sang.

Paris at night
Sylvain killed
Paris in the rain
All this for a dog

When he found Tristan, he asked a single question: 'Did you throw the gun into the Seine?' Without waiting for an answer, he rushed to search Sylvain before letting him in. Sylvain felt palpitations between his legs and barely held back in crushing his fist against Tristan's face.

A few minutes later, Tristan parked the car in front of a construction site. While grabbing Octavo'sbag and a flashlight, he motioned ylvain to follow. They span metal barriers, wade in a sticky slush and took cover behind a construction hut. No risk in being seen. It should be about three in the morning and the rain was still strong. Tristan took a gun out of nowhere, aimed it to Syvain, and said, 'We'll count the bags and check them one by one. If ever I see one open, I'll rip your fucking clothes off, and I'll fuck you until I get my rocks off. Then I'll dump you here. I want no skeletons in my car.'

The bags of pebbles were intact, and Tristan seemed almost disappointed. He was quiet all the whole way home. Apparently he was bored: there were not enough people on the highway at that hour. Once in Puits-

Magdelon he grumbled, jaw wide opened by a loud yawn.

'You'll be paid once we have evidence that Octavo's dead.'

CHAPTER 6

O ctavo's gas-inflated body rose to the surface three days later, under the nose of Japanese tourists who were more excited than upset. On a photo, they were seen smiling and posing proudly, as if they had just won a carp fishing contest.

The restaurateur was identified. His wife had gone to testify.

A newspaper published an article entitled: *'Drugs: a dealer done in.'*

'(...) The French-Brazilian restaurateur, with three bullets in his body was found in the Seine, was working for a drug dealer, following his wife's testimony. However, she said she that had never seen this dealer and knew nothing of it. The investigation continues.

'The role of Octavo B. was to accommodate mules from South America. The mules were ingesting eggs of pure cocaine and traveling with tourist visas to avoid attracting the attention of airport police. Octavo B. and his wife were hosting them in their Paris home for the duration of the visa.

'Octavo B. recovered cocaine eggs excreted by mules and entrusted them to accomplices who are allegedly chemists. Then he would deliver the doses of cocaine and crack to other dealers who were responsible for distribution.

'For some time, he started his own business with his Brazilian network. He used his boss' mules to transport oxidado - a new derivative of cocaine called "oxi" (see article below). He procured them from Brazil for very cheap prices, and then sold them in Paris.

'But Octavo B. went further. He intercepted the deliveries for his boss', and replaced crack stones by oxi pebbles, the appearance of which was similar. Thus, it allowed him to steal his boss' crack, and get it cheaper, the price of oxi.

'According to the wife of Octavo B. "His boss did not see a thing."

'The settlement of accounts suffered by Octavo B. suggested that the boss had finally discovered the cat in the bag... or rather, the shit in the bag.'

Following the article was a second item of an obscure title, but it did not go unnoticed: *The scourge "crack" and "oxi"*

'Oxi, a new derivative of cocaine, has invaded Brazil's major urban centers. From the border of the Amazon regions of Bolivia and Peru, it is the drug that goes up to Brazil. It was also called the "the stone of two Reals" (approximately 0.90€ to a pebble) because of its low price.

'Oxi was a diminutive of oxidado: "rusty" in Portuguese. It has the same shape as crack – a small yellowish stone – and is smoked in an air pipe, the consumer inhaling noxious fumes. Like crack, it has a derivative of based from cocaine, but much more toxic.

'Buyers were trapped as its appearance is identical to the crack. However, the products are different. Crack is made from cocaine dissolved in baking soda or ammonia. The oxi, meanwhile, is a cocaine mixture from oxidized fuel (kerosene, gasoline or fuel oil) mixed with potassium permanganate or lime. There are no special precautions in making it, and it's easy to cook with rudimentary equipment. Its manufacturing cost was lower which explains its rapid spread.

'Those who smoke suffer immediate addiction upon first use, which can sometimes be fatal. The effects are lightning fast: behavioral disorders, vomiting, diarrhea, gingival necrosis, tooth loss, kidney problems. Physical and mental damage is irreversible. Three out of ten victims die within the first year of addiction.

'Experts believe that oxi was poised to replace crack. It is feared that this new scourge would not take a long time to cross further borders.'

The month that just ended was less turbulent for Sylvain. He returned neither to Paris nor to Anvers; neither to Guyana. He resumed his role as a delivery man: seven street deliveries at rue des Rouets for the pantyhose person – 100 Euros for a delivery, as from the beginning. He did not see Edgar Huggins once. Since then, each appointment at the *Bon Bouilleur* was with Martial. The ritual was the same every time: Martial handed him the envelope to deliver and 100 Euros for the previous delivery. Martial, the distinguished Nestor of Huggins Castle, was much less courteous outside its décor – dismissive and unfriendly.

Sylvain studied himself in the mirror while shaving. Black eyes, a straight nose, thick lips, a tanned skin, abundant gray hair with fly-away strands. Nothing to report. Yet the eyes of a painter had transformed his face into artwork. Beauty was in everyone's mind. It could not exist otherwise or elsewhere. That was why the look of one was never the same to that of another.

He recently bought a trailer for his moped. It was more convenient than market strollers to transport plants and sandbags. And then there was Goodboy. The puppy quickly understood: trailer means forest walks. He liked to express his joy by barking, but Sylvain taught him to be quiet. Domestication was easy, as Goodboy was desperate to please his master.

Gauthier's cell phone started ringing. Sylvain listened to the music from elsewhere. It was the first time the phone rang in a while. He followed instructions not to respond immediately and call Gauthier instead.

'Yes, it was me who just called you Mr. Wolf. Are you home?'

'Yes.'

'You will leave immediately! Edgar Huggins has been arrested in his castle with Marie-Jeanne Languerrand, Tristan and Martial. There will be a street raid of Vau-L'Eau. Step on it. Stay away from Puits-Magdelon. If you have cash, do not leave it in the box, hide it away or destroy it. Do not come back until call you.'

Goodboy jumped into the trailer and sat down, face mum, and very proud of him, with compliments and cake. On that May morning, the weather was mild and sullen, the moped made a beeline towards the forest.

Goodboy wore a harness attached to the trailer and watched the landscape scroll by, ears to the wind.

Before leaving the lodge, Sylvain left the window open. If the cops wanted to search, they can return from there without breaking the door. He took the biscuit tin. Money from his sessions with Gadelorge has been spent, but the 2,500 Euros totalling from Huggins' missions were intact. The metal box surrounded by tight plastic tape, can withstand humidity and the assaults of the swarming undergrowth. It will be buried at the foot of a tree. He already knew that.

They walked for an hour when his mobile phone started ringing. Sylvain was ashamed of being the source of the noise against nature in the forest. He cut and called Gauthier back.

'Go back to Rue Vau-L'Eau, Mr. Wolf. Two gendarmes are waiting for you. They will take you to the gendarmerie of Puits-Magdelon saying that it's for an interrogation. I'll be the one handling that, okay?'

'I can't leave my dog alone.'

'I'll keep you at the police time to simulate an interrogation. I'll release you after one hour. Alright?'

'Good. I'll be home in about twenty minutes.'

'Wonderful, Mr. Wolf, the result of our collaboration was great! And I want to commend you for your courage. Ah, the nice haul! The hunt lasted for three years. Huggins was a the missing link. With his arrest, we've greatly crippled the industry. Tristan and Martial are Edgar Huggins' brothers, and Marie-Jeanne

Languerrand is his half-sister. I knew that their castle was a real cache of weapons – a boon for the flagrante delecto. We used it to charge all four of for illegal possession of weapons. Now it will be easy to condemn them permanently after the search of the *Bon Bouilleur* basements, which are full of cocaine, crack, oxi, cannabis, ecstasy and other treats. As for Salvignol Bérengère, who was present at the time of the arrest, she was packed in the same lot. She's Huggins' mistress. We've also nabbed Jeannot Marchadier in his deli and Guylaine Monteil, Maryse Beurdelet and Odon Gadelorge of Rue du Vau-l'Eau; they all dipped in into Huggins' dealership. They're being interrogated as we speak. Long ago I knew exactly who was doing what, but stopping one of the Huggins' heads was a bad tactic. It was imperative to decapitate the hydra starting with their leader, then lop them all off simultaneously.'

Commissioner Gauthier grabbed a water bottle and took a without taking his eyes off of Sylvain. It was too hot in the interrogation room of the gendarmerie – if one can call it a 'room' with its eight square meters. Sylvain was very thirsty.

Gauthier continued.

'Edgar Huggins has imagination. Drug trafficking in such an unimaginable place such as Puits-Magdelon was clever, but he was too greedy. As for you, get ready for the future, because there's always a sequel. Puits-Magdelon is not the hub of a global cocaine trafficking. With Edgar Huggins' arrest, we hold a thread. In pulling it, we hope to unravel the mesh of a network on a larger scale. It will take time – Paris, Guyana, Belgium, South America; the war's just beginning. I need a snitch like you. Your undercover work is irreplaceable.'

Gauthier handed him the bottle. Drinking from the same bottle as Gauthier wasn't appropriate, but Sylvain was too thirsty to refuse.

'I'll give you 5,000 Euros for your past and future cooperation. However, there is one condition: you continue as I ask of you. If you refuse, I'll kick you out in a second. That's my only offer.'

Sylvain held Gauthier's look.

'How much time do I have to give my answer?'

'Immediately, if you want to be released immediately and get your dog. Yes, your friendly dog...'

'Alright!' Sylvain hastily replied.

'All right, Mr. Wolf. I'll take your word. Don't try to escape. You won't go far, and neither will your dog. For the money, I will contact you shortly to give you the location of the appointment. Someone will bring you cash. Do you have a ten- or twenty-Euro bill on you?'

'Yes, I believe so.'

'You'll tear it in two and give half to me for the person who will give you the jackpot. You'll recognize him that way. Might as well use a good old trick – that always works well. Another clarification: this is only the beginning. If you are productive, there will be others, bonanzas like that. As of now, you can't go home. The gendarmes are stationed at Rue du Vau-L'Eau. Once we have received approval, seals will be affixed to the doors of the building. We've gone to get your dog: he's quietly waiting for you in the next room. You go where you want, while staying at my disposal.'

He did not have authority to enter Rue du Vau-L'Eau to take his plants and books. He bought kibble and a bowl for Goodboy. He also brought bottles of water, a picnic basket, and a sleeping bag. The night will soon fall. Sylvain started picking up branches to build a cabin in the forest. Goodboy was having lots of fun.

The green disposable phone still had credits. Now that Huggins and his band were in the shade, he could use it. No. There was another one that never left behind, hidden in the heel of his left boot that he had cobbled skillfully. He dialed a number he knew by heart.

'That's it,' Sylvain said. 'Commissioner Gauthier just offered me 5,000 Euros. That's only the beginning, he said.'

'Good. How will he give you the money?'

Sylvain summarized to Commissioner Lauzanne most of his interview with Commissioner Gauthier.

Once the call was over, he recalled the story of his encounter with Lauzanne, the second commissioner. He met him at the time of the fire from the Avenue de la Gare, just after his first interrogation with Commissioner Gauthier at the gendarmerie of Puits-Magdelon: two commissioners on the same day, and two mobile phones. All fell into place when, after giving Gauthier all he wanted, he felt that he was in an irreversible situation. In fact, with Gauthier, he felt that he got a second blackmailer, and he was too in too deep and too confused mind to find a solution. What was the best choice? Be a slave Edgar Huggins or be the snitch of a police commissioner? From the depths of his heart, the answer came to him: that he, Sylvain Wolf, son of gold smugglers, would collaborate with the police to fight against drug traffickers. This however did not give him his slain childhood back, but he was pleased to participate in the sabotage of whatsoever traffic.

After grueling hours in the mini-interrogation room of the gendarmerie, he took the direction of the Rue du Vau-L'Eau. A few minutes later, he was approached by a young woman dressed for hiking. She asked him his way unfolding a cadastral map. In fact, she took his hand under the map and slipped into an object. It was a cell phone. Agaaaaaain! Sylvain inwardly groaned.

'Go home, now. You will receive a call from the commissioner Lauzanne within twenty minutes,' said the young woman in one breath. 'There will be three rings, then it will stop. You will answer when it rings again. Lauzanne, Commissioner Lauzanne, remember that name.' No sooner said she moved away with smiles and by waving goodbye.

Why would the random meeting with the hiker go unnoticed? From that event, he deduced that it he was not followed and protected by the police, as Gauthier's claimed. When he received the call announced by the false hiker, he listened carefully and asked, 'What proof do I have that you're Commissioner Lauzanne?'

'Your intuition.'

The answer pleased Sylvain. He told him all he knew, all from the beginning.

From that day, Sylvain engaged with conviction in a double agent role – double snitch? – In the service of the police's police.

Lauzanne was commissioner in the Inspection générale de la police nationale, and investigating as such on the Commissioner Gauthier, following suspicions of corruption reported by the gendarmes of Puits-Magdelon.

Shortly before 03:00, he stepped over the cemetery wall, walked among the tombs and entered the mortuary chapel of the Languerrand family. Gendarmes and police united in the same fight would have no trouble welcoming him in.

In his pocket, he had half of a torn 10 Euro bill. Slung over his shoulder, a bag contained 100 halves of 50 Euros. On his head was a stocking. He was a postman at Puits-Magdelon.

He confessed that he was appointed and paid by Commissioner Gauthier.

'Ah, the lovely phone call,' exclaimed the Commissioner Gauthier. Indeed! But probably he had not planned he would be one of the finest catches, as much as his accomplice and enemy, Huggins.

Drug trafficking at Puits-Magdelon: a dirty cop tripping over his own crackdown, read the regional newspaper headline.

In custody, Gauthier played for time. He waited for the fortieth hour to talk to Commissioner Lauzanne. He was indeed an accomplice to Edgar Huggins and his mistress, Bérengère Salvignol, who was call girl in Paris. Gauthier protected the luxury prostitute. In return for his protection and his silence, he dipped his hand on the resale of cocaine to Parisian revelers. Incidentally, he also levied his share from prostitution, more or less in agreement with Huggins.

The matter escalated when Edgar and Bérengère threw him the 'dirty tricks', in Gauthier's words. He decided to take revenge. It was at this time that he made use of Sylvain Wolf to get tips.

Within the shadow of the shadow, Commissioner Lauzanne did the same. The police was alerted by the gendarmes of Puits-Magdelon. They began to suspect a traffic exceeding the sales of grams of cannabis. 'Why didn't Commissioner Gauthier work in collaboration with the drug squad?' They questioned. This was what aroused the suspicion of the police, and therefore, Gauthier went down.

What 'dirty tricks'? Commissioner Lauzanne asked during custody. Gauthier ignored the issue, refusing to say more. How much did the trafficker and the prostitute give him? 10,000 to 12,000 Euros per month? They'll check on it. Were other police officers involved? Not the least of confessions about it.

Within the police of the police, Commissioner Lauzanne and his team did not let the investigation go.

TO BE CONTINUED.

About 30 kilometers from Puits-Magdelon, lies a town of the same size, crossed by a river. He stopped his moped before a gate in wrought iron. Goodboy pawed in the trailer, but waited for Sylvain's to jump off.

A dynamic octogenarian came to greet them, fresh in her sandalwood perfume. She was stunning in her Indian sari in shades of plum and orange. A braid of hair coloured with Henna was raised on top of her head, where five or six strands escaped, as if they were fern leaves.

'You are Mr Sylvain?'

'Yes, Ma'am.'

The old lady began to speak, and her uninterrupted flow was torrential.

'Oooh, such a beautiful dog! He will be happy here! Commissioner Lauzanne told me that I could hire you with eyes closed. Eyes closed? Certainly not! On the contrary, I keep them well open. You know, I don't rely only on my impressions. Incidentally, I immediately saw who you were. You please me already. Commissioner Lauzanne, ah there là là! Pierre is my only son. I did everything to dissuade him from entering the police force! Whatever came to his head! Alas, there was nothing I could do. Follow me, I'll give you a tour of your new home. I've fixed the place up for you. You'll find it comfortable: it's furnished and fully equipped. You'll feel right at him. The big house you see there is my second home. I wished for a year-round caretaker, you see. Supervision, upkeep, and gardening. A vegetable garden, hedges, shrubs, flowers, meadows, woods – would you like that, Mr Sylvain? Wolf Sylvain... Such poetry in your name! Sylvain comes from Latin, *silva*: forest. You are called the Forest Wolf. I'm in love! In fact, I hope that I'm not mistaken! Is "Wolf" your first name? No, don't tell me! For me, it is how it is. You will be called Forest Wolf. I'll call you Wolf. Do I have your permission?'

'Of course, Mrs Lauzanne,' said Sylvain.

A first name? I should have thought about it earlier, said Wolf.

EPILOGUE

Who were the three Huggins brothers? Edgar, Tristan and Martial were the son of Lucien Languerrand and Winona Huggins. Lucien's father was Germain, the cheerful mayor, and of the pious Marie-Jeanne, had been a widower since the birth of his daughter. At Puits-Magdelon, he was the owner of the bistro *Au Bon Bouilleur*, as were his great-grandfather, grandfather and father. He also owned a castle thanks to his maternal ancestry, and was passed on from generation to generation, more and more run down. It had never been inhabited by Languerrand. None had the means to restore it, much less the desire to do so.

Lucien Languerrand met Winona Huggins at a party in a Parisian nightclub. She was a young Native American dancer who worked Paris shows, where she had lived for several years.

Once Germain and Marie-Jeanne reached legal age, Lucien left Puits-Magdelon, joined Winona at the capital and married her. They then lived in Paris where Edgar were born, and the twins, Tristan and Martial.

Winona, a native of Minnesota, introduced her son to the history of the United States. As a priority, it exposed them to horrific episodes of the long extermination of the Indians, their ancestors. Edgar's was much captivated by the adventures of the mafia in Chicago at the time of Prohibition. He was fascinated by the character of Al Capone. As a teenager, he took the habit of dressing like the famous Godfather with his three-piece suit, Borsalino, a trench coat or a cashmere coat. In his young brain, he identified to Al Capone. He was Al Capone.

The Languerrand-Huggins couple made their fortune by opening an American-Native Indian restaurant-tavern Upscale Parisians flocked to the place, until the day when Lucien and Winona died together in a car accident.

In addition to a large fortune divided equally, the three-Huggins-Languerrand inherited a property in Paris and, in turn, Germain and Marie-Jeanne became the owners of *Au Bon Bouilleur*, and the dilapidated castle at Puits-Magdelon with its hectares of woods. Unlike his ancestors, Germain did not revive the bistro, and he remained a farmer and mayor. As for Marie-Jeanne, a homebody and volunteer at the Catholic Relief Services, she was so ashamed of her father that she hastened to use her inheritance for the poor of the parish. 'One way to purify dirty money,' she sighed, eyes to the heavens.

Shortly before dying, Germain confided his fears to a notary, 'I cannot let Marie-Jeanne squander the Languerrand wealth for her charitable works. It is bloodline I hold in high regard. But Marie-Jeanne was the black sheep of the family, and I know she can transform the Puits-Magdelon Castle as reform school for lost sheep.' Thus Germain divided his property between his sister and to the three half-brothers, whose activities he was unaware of. The aim was to entangle Marie-Jeanne in the constraints of unity.

In Paris, the three crooks swimming in the middle of prostitution and drugs. Edgar, worried, thought they were becoming too known, too easily spotted. Also, after Germain's death, they sold their property in Essonne and came to settle in Puits-Magdelon. The restoration of the old Languerrand castle fired up Edgar, who wallowed in the pomp with euphoria. With the lack of a noble title, he invented the status of 'honorary mayor' that captured the curiosity of none other than Sylvain Wolf.

The twins had a poorly finished look and possessed rather low IQs. They were dominated by their older brother. Tristan was a killer and a rapist. Edgar held him in his grip by providing him 'flesh', in the words of Tristan. In addition, there was a carrot: the cars. Tristan was polishing a score in the outbuildings of Puits-Magdelon. Edgar promised him others as often as necessary.

With his brother Martial, it was easier. It was enough to bait him with watches. Martial possessed a collection with value equivalent to tens of thousands of Euros. He spent hours dismantling them... for reassembly.

Their half-sister immediately found herself in a difficult case that urgently needed to be solved. Killing her would be careless. Edgar preferred not to call attention on his brothers and on himself, following their early move to Puits-Magdelon. The three brothers initially locked up Marie-Jeanne in an old cellar of the castle, where the temperature did not exceed 3°C or 4°C. 'I refuse to be complicit in your ignominy!' She yelled for over a night. Faced with such resistance, they threatened the poor of Puits-Magdelon, whom she actively took care of. Marie-Jeanne gave in and did whatever they wanted. To complete her submission to them, they forcefully drugged her for several weeks. In a pitiful state of dependence, she resigned herself to work with them. Tristan took the opportunity: 'If you work nicely with your brothers, I'll rape you.' Marie-Jeanne obeyed, but was raped anyway.

For Edgar, taking cover with his brothers in a backwater town seemed a great idea. Indeed, the disused cellars of the *Bon Bouilleur* became a great storage place for drugs. And the traffic prospered.

Before coming to Puits-Magdelon, Huggins already knew Bérengère Salvignol. A native of Puits-Magdelon, she lived in Paris, where she was a call girl. He began regularly inviting her to his renovated castle. Bérengère was seduced by the lifestyle and Edgar's aristocratic manners. She became his mistress and took a key role as a cocaine purveyor for sinuses of the Parisian jet-setters. Colossal amounts. Trade flourished.

When Bérengère inherited No. 9 of Rue du Vau-L'Eau, Edgar built a plan: to transform the building into the headquarters of dealers. Bérengère immediately saw the profit that she and her lover and she could accumulate. The building was dilapidated and uninhabited for several years, and so she had it renovated, and then looked for tenants.

First Josée Nadar. She was an old concierge of Rue du Vau-L'Eau. A widow who held a maddeningly slim pension, she was the first to accept Bérengère Salvignol's proposal of: a roof over her head for free, and some exceptional bonuses in exchange for small services to the tune of cocaine for an anonymous 'Master'.

To select the other three tenants, Bérengère hand-picked from the list of the long-term unemployed who received no benefits. An accomplice at the employment center provided her with information. Each unemployed 'candidate' was offered free accommodation, together with an offer of paid employment, provided they were in the service of 'Master' and whatever he asked for, whatever his requirements. There was no refusal. The tenants of Rue du Vau-L'Eau did not know that the 'Master' in question was Edgar Huggins. In the building, he was reserved the first floor apartment, as if a supervisor. It was he who developed the circuit of cocaine at Puits-Magdelon, a circuit as tortuous as his mind. Each tenant had his job.

Josée Nadar was responsible for fetching the goods from the butcher, Jeannot Marchadier, at the weekly market. The two, with their reputation as ordinary citizens, were well liked by Huggins. When Salvignol, owner of the deli, proposed to Marchadier to no longer pay the rent, he accepted the deal without flinching. Doses of cocaine transited in his duck confit jars, smuggled and shipped by Octavo from Paris. Josée Nadar recovered jars and handed them to Maryse Beurdelet who transmitted them to his boss.

Bérengère Salvignol convinced one of her networks in Puits-Magdelon – a cocaine addicted lawyer – to hire the said Maryse Beurdelet, who became his private secretary and his drug supplier. The needs were infinite, for him and his 'friends' reached through the Internet. He organized soirées for those who have the taste for sexual fetishism. Their pleasure was purely visual. They gathered to look at each other while their sniffing coke. To look without touching was what excited them. Maryse Beurdelet was not involved in the lawyer's nightlife, but she agreed to show him her ass in private, following two conditions: only during working hours and in exchange for pretty sums of cash. No doubt she ended up liking it because it allowed her to come up with a clever ploy to attract Sylvain Wolf in the attic and get peeped at naked in her bathroom – for free, too.

On his part, Guylaine Monteil specialized in crack cocaine and cannabis. Bérengère Salvignol had found her a job at the municipal library. The objective was to hook teenagers, practically children. Guylaine Monteil hid drugs in books of her choosing. Upon appointment and payment in advance, she pointed out the relevant titles to 'subscribers' who fetched their merchandise discreetly. It was Edgar Huggins' idea, of which he was very proud. Indeed, the comings and goings of high school students at the library – she even began to be known to some insiders in the surrounding towns – were never suspected by anyone.

As to the third-floor tenant, Odon Gadelorge received parcels from Paris, sent by the indispensable Octavo. They contained cocaine concealed in paint tubes. Bérengère Salvignol had gotten him a position as a painting instructor for adults. At first, she sent fake students to Gadelorge, who were true cocaine buyers. Word of mouth did the rest. Coke transited during classes or through the tubes of paint.

The postman who delivered the package to Gadelorge ay Rue du Vau-L'Eau was in on it as well. It was this same postman who was stopped in the cemetery of Puits-Magdelon with his bag full of Euros for Sylvain Wolf, by the Commissioner Gauthier. How was Gauthier childish enough to stage such a scenario?

For the position of caretaker, a profile was reported appropriately to Bérengère Salvignol by her accomplice at the employment center. Sylvain Wolf was, too, a long-term unemployed. Gardener, aged fifty-nine, he was wandering in the city, the prefectural located about sixty kilometers from Puits-Magdelon, with the hope of finding odd jobs. His resources were so weak that he was homeless for more than a year.

When Sylvain Wolf began his new job, Edgar Huggins wondered how he was going to use this new Concierge – an interesting character to use, discrete, unrelated, unknown. Then there was the murder of Josée Nadar, a custom blackmail, supplied by Sylvain Wolf himself. A godsend.

Some Magdelonais crack cocaine and cannabis consumers were also dealers. Thus, the squatters at Avenue La Gare declared a gang war. This resulted in Sylvain Wolf's impossible deliveries, brought about by a gang from a neighboring town of Puits-Magdelon, attempting to bypass the organization in place and steal drugs. Rival gangs clashed and drama ensued: there was the fire and murder of two young Guyanese burned alive. For once, Edgar Huggins had no hand in it.

Following the case, Huggins wanted to get rid of both unwanted witnesses who saw Sylvain at Avenue de La Gare.

First Brueil Sabine, wife of the notary. She had had the misfortune in seeing Sylvain Wolf, and the bad idea to tell the police. Tristan was commissioned to make her disappear. He took the opportunity to rape her and then finished her with kitchen knives. Tristan had his brother Edgar's permission to violate every person he shot, man or woman. 'Flesh,' he rambled.

At the time of the crime, her husband, Pierre-Louis Breuil, participated in one of fetish evenings of the lawyer. As expected, the worthy notary wanted to cover up his sexual fantasies and his cocaine addiction. As a result, his alibi crumbled. Thus he was suspected of murdering his wife and then remanded in custody. The lawyer visited him in prison and put pressure on him to not reveal anything of his famous parties. He terrorized him by threatening to bring minors in the world of drugs, which effectively silenced the notary. However, when questioned, Maryse Beurdelet unpacked all the story and the lawyer was arrested in turn.

After the murder of Sabine Breuil, there was that of Florent Marchadier. He testified, too, against Sylvain Wolf. He should not have. In prison, two prisoners contacted by Tristan did the work: they staged asuicide by hanging Florent and were paid doses of coke. Florent's father, Jeannot the butcher, was seized with madness, 'I'll turn you in, Salvignol. You, and your god damned master!' Tristan undertook the task of silencing him. No one ever knew how, but it was radical. And Jeannot Marchadier continued to peddle his duck confit jars à la cocaine.

In fact, Edgar thought he was clever with Bérengère. He wanted to build a 'decentralized regional traffic from the capital,' he explained to her. Then he added:

'It's like radar controls. There's less risk of being found out on a provincial level than national.' Wrong! For Mr. Huggins was nabbed on the country road leading to the castle.

Beyond Puits-Magdelon, Sylvain Wolf's information enabled other arrests.

Malcolm was rightfully grilled by Guyanese police to release the names of his two accomplices at the Cayenne-Rochambeau Airport. The police did not give up eliciting further information on those of Paris-Orly. They kept Malcolm warm in his overcrowded cell and pursued the investigation, in collaboration with the metropolis.

As for Jasper, the Anvers man in a wheelchair, was followed and monitored for some time by the sleuths of the drug squad, who had a good lead: the prostitute at Antwerpen-Centraal. In agreement with the French police, the Belgian police awaited the arrest of Edgar Huggins to jump on Jasper. It was done.

In Paris, the wily Octavo was unknown to the police. The man Sylvain Wolf had killed and thrown into the Seine was not just an essential link in the traffic. Huggins also paid for the silence of mules that landed in South America, force-fed cocaine eggs. Octavo assessed smugglers upon arrival. Those he considered too emotional were systematically eliminated as they were likely to be noticed at airports check-points. Traumatized by their first visit, they were not always able to make a second, and in that case, Octavo avoided putting the network at risk, especially that smugglers were often charged with ecstasy for the return trip. Indeed, the colored tablets exported nicely.

The loss of a mule mattered little to dealers. Requests poured in and the workforce was inexhaustible. No one reported the disappearance of smugglers. No one claimed them. Threatened with horrors on their children, the families were silent. These smugglers were from lost jungle villages not even listed on maps, or were from urban slum areas. The sum of money promised was such that they could not assess them mentally. They were all volunteers. Many only went on a one way trip. The dreamed about Eldorado disintegrated as fast as they did.

For those who were stopped at airports, prison was inevitable, sometimes served a sentence that lasted years. Yet Justice knew that the exemplary punishment of the underlings was an injustice. Poverty led them to gamble everything and anything. Society, not content in just starving them, had found nothing better than to repress them. That did not create any ripples in the world and did not move them a nano-millimetre closer towards winning the war against drug trafficking.